Matt Cartney

Red, White and Black

A Danny Lansing Adventure

To Mya,

Don't try this at home!

Matt Cartney.

www.stridentpublishing.co.uk

Matt Cartney

Red,

and

A Dann

White Black

Lansing Adventure

WWW.DANNYLANSING.COM

Published by
Strident Publishing Ltd
22 Strathwhillan Drive
The Orchard, Hairmyres
East Kilbride G75 8GT

Tel: +44 (0)1355 220588
info@stridentpublishing.co.uk
www.stridentpublishing.co.uk

A catalogue record for this book is
available from the British Library.

ISBN 978-1-905537-34-1

The publisher acknowledges subsidy from
Creative Scotland towards the publication of this volume.

Typeset in Bembo by LawrenceMann.co.uk
Cover image © LawrenceMann.co.uk 2012
Printed by Cox & Wyman

ALBA | CHRUTHACHAIL

FOR THE AGENTS,
THE COMMANDOS, THE PILOTS.
FOR ALL THOSE WHO DID NOT,
AND DO NOT, STAND IDLY BY.

MATT CARTNEY

When he's not working and writing, Matt Cartney is an intrepid traveller, mountaineer and snow-boarder. His love of adventure is infectious; presenting in schools, bookshops and libraries he includes photographs and stories of his exploits from around the world. He is always willing to try new things, whether it is cycle touring in Australia, skiing across a Norwegian mountain range or attempting to ride his motorcycle to Nepal (an attempt cut short by terrorists in Baluchistan).

Matt lives in Edinburgh. *Red, White and Black* is the second novel in the Danny Lansing series, following on from the success of *The Sons of Rissouli*. If you would like him to present at your school, you can email him on mail@dannylansing.com

PROLOGUE

HARDANGER PLATEAU, NORWAY.
FEBRUARY 1945.

Torn fragments of moonlit cloud formed a broken ceiling at about six thousand feet. Beyond, the sky was clear and full of glittering stars. They would be coming tonight, the conditions were perfect.

Knut wriggled his toes in his boots and stamped his skis down into the snow one more time. Even for someone used to Norwegian winters it was bitterly cold and the young agent was troubled by the lack of feeling in his hands and feet. Hopefully the British would be on time — he didn't want to have to wait out here for long.

There were three of them standing there; leaving long, grey shadows in the moonlight. Around them, as far as the eye could see, stretched the rolling undulations and broken crags of the Hardangervidda. The whole mountain plateau was white with snow; even its lakes, frozen solid for the winter, lay under the frigid blanket. Indeed, the lakes up here carried such a thickness of ice you could land an aeroplane on them.

It was this fact, coupled with the spectacular isolation, that had led them to ski through the night to this particular location. Somewhere above, making his lonely way through the darkness, an RAF pilot would be steering his aircraft to the same spot in the endless wilderness.

The German had arrived in Rjukan two weeks before. No-one would have guessed that the grey-haired man who had stepped off the bus from Oslo was a Generalleutnant in the German Air Force. Dressed in a worn blue suit and moving with the hunched shuffle of the tired and defeated, he appeared every bit the French electrical engineer his identity papers said he was. When Knut and Arne had met him by the church, he had looked strangely forlorn — a soldier shorn of his uniform and exiled from his country. The men he'd spent five and a half years fighting were now his only friends.

That same night they had taken the German to Arne's house, where they had equipped him with warm clothing, skis and a white camouflage ski-suit. By midnight they were climbing out of Rjukan, on a steep trail through the trees, to the barren isolation and tenuous freedom of the plateau.

They had spent much of the next fourteen days stormbound in a tiny hut in the south of the Hardangervidda. The weather had closed in, bringing savage winds that had howled around the hut both night and day. So much snow had built up against the windward side that it had blocked out the window. They had gone outside only to go to the toilet and to collect more snow to melt for cooking and drinking. These trips were made as brief as possible; the cold was so intense that hypothermia would set in very quickly and exposed skin would freeze in a few minutes.

During those long days, huddled round the old wood-burning stove and trying to eke out their meagre rations, the Norwegians had started to get to know their German charge. He spoke little of the war or of his role in it. He rarely mentioned the Nazis and he spoke only briefly of what had made him defect to the allies. Not once did he allude to the contents of the heavy briefcase that never left his side. And because the Norwegians did not need to know, they did not ask.

He did talk about the town in Bavaria where he'd grown up, however. There had been a cavernous beer-hall in the main square, an ancient church and a beautiful girl who worked at the library. A concerted campaign of wooing had made that girl his wife. He had not seen her for nearly two years. Now he wondered if he would ever see her again.

Knut, despite himself, had begun to like the German. He was a tough, gruff old soldier; with the ramrod posture and measured mannerisms of German aristocracy. Yet below the martial exterior was a human being. A glimmer of humanity remained, despite his years serving the Nazi regime.

The breaking point had come when he had been posted to the camp at Nordhausen. What he had seen there had revolted him. His hatred of the Nazis had finally overcome his love of Germany and he had fled — taking with him all the information he could gather that would be useful to the allies. His rank and position meant that information was worth a great deal. That was why the allies were sending a plane: he was a valuable asset.

There was no wind — not the slightest whisper to mask the sound of an approaching aircraft. The silence was so complete that Knut could hear his breath as it rushed from his lungs to hang in white clouds in the freezing air. At least they should be able to hear the British coming. Suddenly, there it was: a wavering hum that came and went, right on the edge of earshot. The sound became gradually deeper, building to a reverberating drone that seemed outrageously loud in the stillness of the night.

Knut and Arne sprang into action. Skiing out across the frozen lake they distributed three lights in a triangle, pointing out the direction in which the plane should land.

The first they saw of the aeroplane was a tiny shadow flitting between the clouds — like a nervous sparrow hiding from hawks. Shortly, the shadow turned in their direction; the landing lights had been spotted.

There was nothing they could do but watch. It was a tense moment: a dangerous landing on a frozen lake in enemy-occupied territory. The slightest mishap could spell disaster. The hunched silhouette of the RAF Lysander approached in a long, flat turn, bringing it in line with the makeshift runway. It sank to the snow in a graceful flop, bouncing lightly on its skis before sliding gradually to a halt; the airscrew ripping up a cloud of powder snow in its wake. Wasting no time, the pilot turned the aircraft around and taxied over to where the three men stood.

The German had taken off his skis and was already striding towards the aircraft by the time it reached them. The pilot did not try to shout over the noise of his engine and merely pointed him in the direction of the rear cockpit. The German threw his briefcase in first then clambered up after it. Before closing the cockpit he turned and looked over at the two Norwegians. He shouted something, but the battering slipstream of the airscrew flung his words into oblivion. Knut held his hand to his ear to signal that they had not heard, but it was pointless. The German smiled and shrugged, then saluted them and banged the cockpit closed.

Opening the Lysander's throttle, the pilot swung the aircraft round and it was soon racing tail-up across the frozen lake. Knut and Arne grinned at each other as it lifted off and turned to the south-west. They were still congratulating each other on a job well done, when a snarling roar ripped through the night and a black shadow flashed over their heads. Knut grabbed Arne's shoulder in alarm and pointed:

"A Junkers! The Germans…"

He was interrupted by the heavy thumping of the twin-engined night fighter's cannon as it opened fire on the Lysander; yellow streaks of tracer drawing bright lines in the darkness. The Lysander stood little chance, it was outpaced, outgunned and taken completely by surprise. Knut and Arne watched in horror as a spark of flame flared in the sky, then fell, disappearing into the snows.

They started immediately, skiing as quickly as they could over the moonlit snow. It was nearly two kilometres to the crash site but they reached it eventually, breathing hard from the fastest skiing either of them had ever done. The Lysander seemed to have survived the crash quite well; the undercarriage had collapsed and there were many large holes torn in its fuselage by the canon fire, but it had not lost its wings and it lay in an upright position. It looked as though the pilot had managed to pull off some kind of landing. Knut held his breath as he approached the cockpit, daring to hope that they might find the occupants alive.

The German sat strapped tightly into his seat, his hands still gripping the handle of the briefcase that lay on his lap. His head, however, had been hit by a cannon round and had disintegrated, leaving just a stump of neck sticking out of his camouflage ski suit.

The pilot appeared to have fared little better. As Knut and Arne forced open the cockpit, they saw a lifeless form in a sheepskin flying jacket, lying with his head flung back and his mouth open. An ugly wound ran across the left side of his forehead. As Knut reached down to feel for a pulse in the pilot's neck, however, a low groan escaped the ashen lips.

"Are you all right?" said Knut.

The pilot groaned again and his eyes flickered open for the briefest of moments.

"What? Who the devil…" he whispered before losing consciousness again; his head rolling backwards as limp as a rag doll's.

"Hey! Stay awake, you! Stay alive!" Knut shouted, willing the pilot to cling on to life.

A sudden thought came to him and he pushed a hand down the man's collar, pulling out his dog-tags. He looked down and read the fibre disc lying on his glove: 'Lansing, D.' There was a number and then 'RAF'.

"Hey! Lansing! Wake up! Do not die here!" The pilot stirred, his eyes opening again. He peered at Knut dully, as though trying to work out who he was.

"That's better!" said Knut. "You have been shot down, but do not worry. My friend and I will get you to safety!"

CHAPTER ONE

DUNKELD, SCOTLAND.
THE PRESENT DAY

Danny looked about furtively to see if he was being watched. He couldn't see any sign of the law on the deserted, riot-torn streets, but then, that didn't mean they weren't hiding somewhere nearby. He checked out the car again; a 1971 Ford Torino Cobra. Pretty cool. Not too hard to break into either. That was the great thing about 1970s security; effectively it didn't exist. Hotwiring should be a breeze too.

He flexed his outrageously muscular arms, causing his elaborate prison tattoos to ripple and distort, and laughed. It was a sneering, phlegmy laugh of triumph that echoed eerily from the concrete walls of the underpass. Oh yeah, he was going to boost himself a real sweet ride. Once he'd done that, he was going to stick up the orphanage round the corner…

His concentration was broken by a knock at his bedroom door.

"Come in."

"Hey Danny... Jings are you still playing that flippin' computer game? You realise the sun is shining on the other side of those curtains? I am this close..." Angus held his thumb and forefinger a few millimetres apart, "...to giving you a box of matches, the log-splitting axe and the keys to my motorbike, just to get you to go outside."

Danny laughed. "It was raining the last time I looked!"

"That was three hours ago!" said Angus. "Anyway, that's not why I came up. There is someone here who wants to meet you."

"Oh, okay." Danny threw his games console joy-pad aside and followed Angus downstairs. He was intrigued; Angus hadn't said who was waiting in their living-room, but something about his manner suggested it was someone interesting.

In fact, there were two people waiting to see him. A robust, friendly-looking lady in middle age and a much older man whose once considerable height was now compromised by a pronounced stoop. As Angus disappeared into the kitchen, the lady stepped forward to shake Danny's hand.

"Hello Daniel. It's lovely to meet you. My father and I are in Scotland on holiday. He trained here during the war and wanted to come back for a little nostalgia trip. We thought, while we were here, we would pay you a visit. I hope you don't mind, my father was very keen to meet you." She spoke perfect English, but her accent had the soft, resonant tone of a Northern European. Danny guessed she might be German or Dutch.

"Um… no, I don't mind. It's nice to meet you." He thought frantically, trying to work out who these people might be, but he drew a blank. "Sorry, I'm not sure…"

"I knew your great-grandfather," the old man said, realising some explanation was called for. His accent had the same gentle timbre and his English was equally perfect. "I believe you are named after him?"

"Yes, I was named after my great-granddad, Daniel Lansing."

The old man gazed at him from under wildly bushy, snow-white eyebrows. His eyes were the blue of glacial ice and seemed to Danny to be reading him like a book. Not just seeing the mop-headed youth in scruffy jeans and snack-damaged t-shirt, but assessing his very character, determining his strengths and gauging his intelligence.

"Yes. I see your great-grandfather in you. I

think you share the same qualities." He smiled. "And I don't just mean the colour of your hair!"

Danny was pleased; his great-granddad had won the DSO in the Second World War.

"Thanks. My dad told me he was a hero."

"He was indeed." The old man smiled again, his eyes unfocused now, as he recalled some ancient memory. "However, I am forgetting myself…" He held out a hand in introduction. "My name is Knut Jorgensen and I am from Bergen, in Norway. Your great-grandfather and I were good friends."

Shaking the proffered hand, Danny suddenly remembered his manners.

"Sorry, Mr Jorgensen. Please have a seat." He indicated the scruffy leather couch lurking under a painting of a mountain. "Would you like a cup of tea?"

"Way ahead of you, Danny!" said Angus, returning through the kitchen door, carrying a tray of tea and biscuits. Once they had all settled down, poured themselves a cuppa and balanced custard creams on their knees, Danny asked the obvious question:

"How did you know my great-granddad?"

And so Knut told them how he had been a secret agent during the war and how he and his friend Arne had been given the job of taking the German and his secrets into the mountains, so that he could be picked up by a British aeroplane. He told them how Danny's great-grandfather had been the pilot of the Lysander that had been sent for the German. How it had been shot down, just after take-off, and how he and Arne had carried the wounded pilot to safety and hidden him in a remote hut until he had recovered. He also told them how Flight Lieutenant Daniel Lansing DSO had then joined the Norwegian resistance and spent the rest of the war fighting alongside them.

"We became great friends in those final months of the war," Knut concluded. "After it was all over we kept in touch. A few months before he died, he wrote to tell me how his grandson had named his new-born son after him. He was very proud."

Danny was amazed. He had known his great-grandfather had been a bit of a character, but this was incredible. It turned out he was not only a decorated pilot, but a resistance fighter as well!

They talked for over two hours, a host of fascinating stories coming to light; some heroic, some funny, some terribly tragic. Knut seemed happy to tell the tales and Danny and Angus were a willing audience.

It was one thing to read about these things in books, quite another to hear it from the lips of someone involved. Eventually Knut's daughter interrupted the storytelling.

"We must go, father," she said, glancing at her watch. "We must catch dinner at the hotel."

"Ah! Yes, you are right, my dear. Well, it has been nice to meet you, Daniel. I feel you are a chip off the old block!"

"It's been very interesting to meet you, Mr Jorgensen. I hope you enjoy the rest of your holiday."

"I'm sure I will!"

As the old man rose to put on his coat, Danny stood up and, a little red in the face, asked the question that he had been burning to ask for several minutes.

"Mr Jorgensen... I was wondering, the secrets the German was carrying, what happened to them? Did you ever get them back to Britain?"

"What? Oh... no. We could not carry a wounded man and the briefcase; it was too heavy and Daniel was our priority. We buried it on the plateau. German mountain troops searched the area around the crashed Lysander for weeks, looking for Daniel, meaning it was too risky to go back and get it.

After that," he shrugged, "we were too concerned with the liberation of Norway to worry about some briefcase full of papers. It is probably still there!"

Danny's lips curled into a slow, cat-like smile of intrigue.

"Really! Do you think you could remember where?"

Angus chuckled quietly to himself, he knew exactly what his nephew was thinking.

Knut looked briefly at the ceiling, as though ordering his thoughts.

"Yes, even after all these years, I can tell you exactly where we buried it! Of course, I thought we would be returning for it, so I made sure to memorise its location. It is under a boat-shaped rock, three hundred and twenty metres due west of the crash site of the Lysander."

Angus looked at Danny and grinned.

"Let me guess. You want to go to Norway for your Easter holidays?"

"Do you think you could get a magazine article out of it?"

"Undoubtedly. It's not the kind of thing I usually write about, but it will make a nice change from being shot at by gangsters…"

Red, White & Black

Just two weeks later Danny found himself on the Hardanger plateau. They had flown to Oslo from Edinburgh the day after his school had broken up for the holidays and had spent only one night in Norway's capital. Just enough time to stock up on food and fuel for their stove. Early the next morning they had caught a bus to the town of Rjukan.

From there, they had climbed a steep, zigzag trail through the surrounding forest, emerging from the tree-line in the late afternoon, with only a couple of hours of daylight in which to find a place to camp.

As they left the last stunted firs behind them and climbed onto the barren plateau, Danny looked around at the vast, empty landscape. The Hardangervidda seemed to stretch on forever — an endless, undulating wilderness of snow and ice. This was, he knew, Europe's largest mountain plateau. A different world, three thousand feet above his own, frozen in an Arctic chill for six months of the year.

They were planning to spend a week up on the plateau. Angus thought this would be sufficient time to find whatever remained of the crashed Lysander and (fingers crossed) the briefcase full of secrets which he hoped would provide him with a story. If they didn't find the briefcase, he reasoned, they would still have had a fine adventure in one of Europe's most unspoilt environments.

They knew the Hardangervidda to be a beautiful place, but also uncompromisingly harsh. To survive up there they needed to be prepared. Their packs were laden with goose-down sleeping bags, a geodesic mountaineering tent, warm clothing, a snow-shovel, a snow-saw, a mountain of high energy food and a stove to cook it on. Fortunately, over the years, Angus had acquired enough gear to equip both of them. Some of it had seen better days, but it was all serviceable enough.

They skied in silence; absorbing the wild beauty of their environment. There was no sound other than the faint rustling of the wind as it rushed over the delicate, wind-carved ridges of snow that covered the plateau. Angus told him these ridges were called sastrugi and Danny made a mental note to remember the name so he could use it to impress his mates the next time his uncle took them mountaineering in Scotland.

A sky of thin, silvery clouds stretched overhead, turning the world into a monochrome vision of pristine isolation. The light was fading and the pale yellow sun was dipping towards the horizon when Angus finally broke the hush.

"This looks like a good spot," he said, indicating a flat area of snow sheltered from the wind by a low crag. "Why don't you get the stove going while I pitch the tent?" This sounded like a good deal to Danny.

Angus cleared a space a little bigger than the tent by stomping the snow down with his skis. He then took the skis off and pitched the tent, securing it with over-sized snow pegs and tying its guy-lines round their skis and ski-poles, which he had driven into the snow. He then used his snow-saw to cut some large, square blocks out of a nearby drift. These he stacked in a crude wall around the tent, as extra protection from the elements.

After a few minutes, Danny finally got the stove working and managed to melt enough snow for a couple of mugs of tea. The water was just coming to the boil as Angus put the finishing touches to his protective wall.

They stood outside for a while, watching the sun disappear below the western horizon and warming their hands on their mugs of tea. As the stars began to appear in the sky to the east, the temperature dropped sharply and the relative warmth of the tent beckoned.

After a large dinner of pasta with tomato sauce and smoked fish (Danny would come to get very bored of this meal) they settled down to read for a while before going to sleep. Wrapped in the soft folds of his sleeping bag, Danny felt curiously satisfied. Something about the simplicity of their comforts — hot food, shelter, warm beds — compared to the harshness of the environment outside, made those comforts seem all the greater. He was lying in a sleeping bag on a thin foam mat, in twelve degrees of frost and protected from the elements by a couple of layers of nylon; yet he had a feeling of comfort and security that could not be matched by a soft bed in a warm house. Within minutes, he had surrendered to a deep and dreamless sleep.

Danny lay in his sleeping bag the following morning with an overwhelming feeling of reluctance. It was lovely and warm inside his bag and unbelievably freezing outside. There were no two ways about it.

Inside: cosier than a puppy's navel. Outside: colder than the dark side of the moon. However, at some point he was going to have to get up and go for a pee. A muffled voice came from the sleeping bag next to him.

"Do you know where the expression 'cold enough to freeze the balls off a brass monkey' comes from?"

"No, but I've a feeling you're about to tell me."

"It's a Royal Navy expression. On the old sailing ships they used to keep their cannon balls on a rack called a 'brass monkey'. In really cold weather the rack would contract and the cannon balls would fall off…"

"You are full of useless information. What's for breakfast? I've got a horrible feeling you're going to say 'warm muesli'."

Angus thought for a second. "Hmm…warm muesli."

An hour later they had struck camp and were off, skiing west-north-west under a cloudless sky. It was bitterly cold and they had to wear all of their clothes in order to keep warm.

As the sun rose in the sky, however, it started to get warmer and by late morning they had replaced gloves and hats with sun-cream and stripped off a few layers of clothing. Soon, they were skiing along in perfect conditions; firm snow below and a windless, blue sky above.

They made good time, covering eight kilometres before stopping for lunch. Climbing a craggy hillock, which commanded fantastic views in all directions, they set down their heavy packs to sit on.

"What sort of article are you going to write, then?" asked Danny, through a mouthful of cheese and crackers.

"Well, that depends on what we find," replied Angus. "If we do find the briefcase, it could contain some fascinating stuff. Remember that several men risked their lives trying to get those documents to Britain. There's bound to be something of interest in there.

"Of course, it all happened a long time ago, so it's unlikely to contain secrets that are still unknown. At some stage, they will have come to light in other ways. However, it would still be a very interesting find. I doubt I'd have any trouble selling an article. Hopefully there will be enough left of the Lysander for some nice photos. Tell you what, you can earn your cheese and crackers by taking some photos if you like. You can use my camera; I'll give you a few pointers on how to use it this evening."

"Cool. I'd definitely be up for that." It was great to be on this expedition, just for the experience of being on the Hardangervidda, but the idea that he might contribute to Angus's article made the whole thing even more exciting. He would love to see photos that he had taken printed in a magazine.

The afternoon continued fine and they made good progress, reaching their campsite in plenty of time to pitch the tent before dark.

After dinner, Angus gave him his promised tutorial on the use of the camera. He took a few practice shots of the tent in its beautiful wilderness location and a few more of the watery winter sunset. Finally retreating to his sleeping bag, he read less than half a page of his book before falling into an exhausted slumber.

The noise of the tent as it flapped and rippled in a stiff morning breeze woke him. Yawning, he looked over to find out if Angus was conscious yet, an empty sleeping bag giving him his answer. At that moment there was a crunching of footsteps outside and the tent's door unzipped noisily.

A red-faced and grinning Angus appeared, pushing a steaming bowl in Danny's direction.

"Breakfast!" he said.

"Warm muesli?"

"Warm muesli."

"Next time *I* choose what we bring for breakfast, Okay?"

"Nothing sets you up for the day like a bowl of warm muesli."

"True. If your plan is to spend the day trying to suppress your gag reflex."

"Do you want a cuppa?"

"Anything that will wash away the taste of wrinkly fruit and bakery floor-sweepings will be very welcome."

"Industry standard?"

"Yes please."

It took much less time to strike camp, as it always does on the second day of an expedition. They were hoping to reach the site of the crashed Lysander by noon, so the quick start was a good thing. It was windier than it had been the day before, but the sky was still blue as they set out on their journey.

"Be careful," said Angus. "This wind makes the risk of frostbite much greater. Make sure none of your skin is exposed for long, or it could freeze solid. When the fluid in your flesh freezes, it expands, like the water in an ice-cube tray. That destroys the cells your flesh is made from and the frozen body part goes black, dies and falls off."

"Lovely!"

"Although, to be wholly accurate, it will often need to be snipped off with a pair of scissors."

"Really."

"If you leave it dangling it can go gangrenous, swell up and start weeping pus."

"Okay... will keep my hat and gloves on."

"And the smell is just horrendous... sticks to the back of your throat like accidentally inhaled snot. I remember once in Alaska..."

"I get the picture! Now, can we please go and look for this crashed aeroplane?"

For the next two hours they skied north, to the lake the Lysander had reportedly crashed beside. Reaching its eastern end, they descended to its frozen surface and continued along the snow-covered ice to the West. The only thing that indicated that they were skiing over the surface of a lake was the perfect flatness of the snow; apart from that, the white blanket remained exactly the same.

"Knut said that there is an inlet at the western end, which points north. The remains of the Lysander should be about a hundred metres north of the end of that inlet," said Angus, pointing at the far end of the lake. It looked a long way, but they covered the distance surprisingly quickly and were soon close to where the inlet should be. After a brief search Danny saw what they were hunting for: a narrow area of flat snow that stretched northwards from the main body of the lake.

"There it is!" he said, skiing off without waiting for Angus. He was very excited; they seemed incredibly close to what they had come so far to find. Somewhere under this white blanket lay the wreckage of an aeroplane that his own great-grandfather had been flying when it had been shot down. An aeroplane which was inextricably linked to a story of heroism, espionage and war. An aeroplane whose crash site might help them find a briefcase full of secrets that had lain undisturbed for over sixty years.

At the end of the inlet the ground rose gently towards a conical summit about four hundred metres away. A number of rounded lumps in the snow scattered the area, but none of them looked like an aeroplane. Danny was disappointed.

"It doesn't look like there is an aeroplane under the snow anywhere near here," he said.

"I wouldn't say that," replied Angus. "There's a lot of humps and bumps under the snow that could be bits of wreckage. Were you expecting to find a complete aeroplane?"

"I dunno, I hadn't really thought about it. I guess so."

"I'm afraid that was never going to happen. A lot of it will have been taken as salvage and some of what was left will have corroded away. Some of it might even have sunk into the ground; it's pretty boggy here in the summer. Having said that, a fair amount of it should still be lying about. Low value stuff or things that were damaged in the crash would not have been salvaged. Of course, some parts would just be too heavy to move; the engine for instance."

"So, are we going to dig up every one of these lumps till we find the plane?"

"I'm afraid so."

"That's a lot of work."

"Yes. Aren't you glad you had a great big bowl of warm muesli for breakfast?"

Danny surveyed the area with distaste. There were dozens of lumps and bumps and the remains of the

Lysander could be under any of them. They would have to dig away at least a foot of snow each time, to discover whether a lump contained a boulder, a hummock of frozen heather, or a 1940's aero engine. They could be digging away for days before they found anything. A sudden thought came to him.

"I've got a better idea! Aeroplanes are made of iron and steel, right?"

"Well, they are made mostly from aluminium, but there will be quite a lot of parts, particularly in the engine, made of iron or steel."

"And iron and steel are magnetic, right?"

"Yes, they are."

"In which case, couldn't we just hold a compass next to each lump of snow until we find one that pulls the compass needle towards it?"

Angus looked at Danny and grinned.

"Danny... you are a genius!"

Dividing the search area into two, they began a systematic hunt for the Lysander. Starting where the lake met the shore, they moved slowly northwards, checking every hump of snow for the slightest magnetism. For some time they found nothing, the needles of their compasses pointing resolutely north. At last, however, about eighty metres from the lake-shore, Danny struck gold. Bending down to hold his compass next to a particularly large mound, he noticed the needle deflect slightly to the left. It was a barely noticeable movement, but there was no doubt about it; whatever lay under this pile of snow was magnetic.

"Hey! Angus!" he shouted, waving excitedly. "I've got something!"

"Great! I'll be right over!"

Even before Angus had finished sliding to a halt, he was taking off his pack so that he could get to the snow-shovel strapped to its side. He was soon attacking the hummock with it, lifting off great scoops of snow every second. Soon, there came the sound they had been waiting for; the scraping clunk of the shovel hitting something metal.

Clearing away the snow with his hands, Angus uncovered a rounded piece of corroded metal.

"Looks like a cylinder head," he said.

"A what?"

"A cylinder head. It's part of an engine. If my guess is right, there should be another one right about… here."

He pushed the blade of the shovel into the snow to be rewarded with another metallic clunk.

"Yes! What we have here…" he said, grinning at Danny, "…is a Bristol Mercury nine-cylinder rotary engine."

"Out of a Lysander?"

"Out of a Lysander."

As Angus continued to dig the remains of the aeroplane out of the snow, Danny took photographs. At last, when Angus tired, Danny picked up the shovel and continued digging. It was surprisingly hard work, but incredibly exciting. Soon, they had uncovered the engine and much of the cockpit. A little more work and the whole aircraft (or what was left of it) was laid out before them. All the instruments and controls had been removed, but the cockpit and most of the fuselage remained. It appeared to have sunk several feet into the peaty soil, which was why it had not made a larger hummock in the snow. There was no sign of the wings, nor of the tail.

"Well, here it is. My great-granddad's Lysander!" said Danny. In that moment, staring at the corroded and bullet-torn fuselage, he felt incredibly proud. His great-granddad had climbed into this tiny, fragile machine and flown it across the North Sea at night, through murderous coastal defences, to land on a frozen lake high in the Norwegian mountains.

At the same time, millions of men and women all over Europe had been risking their lives in a similar manner. Not for personal gain, fame or fortune, but for the greater good — to defeat an evil that threatened to engulf the whole world. He shivered, but whether it was due to the cold or this sudden insight into the heroism of his great-grandfather's generation, he wasn't sure.

He took some more photos and poked around the wreckage for a while, reluctant to leave this connection to his family history. Eventually, however, he realised they had to get a move on; the afternoon was getting old and the temperature was dropping as the light was fading. Clouds were moving in from the north and a cold wind started to whip up flurries of spindrift. He looked over to where Angus was standing.

"You ready?" his uncle asked. Danny nodded. "Then let's go and find that briefcase!"

Taking a bearing of two hundred and seventy degrees, or due west, from the wreckage, they started to pace out the three hundred and twenty metres to where the boat-shaped rock should be. They backed up their pacing using a GPS, to make sure their navigation was as accurate as possible. They had no idea how Knut had measured the distance between the Lysander and the rock sixty-seven years ago and they had no idea how accurate that measurement might be, so they kept a look out for promising lumps in the snow as they walked.

When they reached a distance of exactly three hundred and twenty metres from the wreckage, they looked at each other and laughed. Right in front of them was an oval bulge of snow about a metre long and thirty centimetres higher than its surroundings. Knut's measurement was bang on.

Once they had cleared the snow from around the boulder, they could see that it was indeed perfectly boat shaped. It looked like a miniature version of the kind of squat rowing boat that fishermen use to collect lobster pots in the Western Isles of Scotland. It also looked extremely heavy.

"There's a hernia waiting to happen, if ever I've seen one," commented Angus. "I wonder how Knut and his mate moved it in 1945."

"Could we use a ski as a lever?" asked Danny. He had recently been forced by his physics teacher to sit through a television documentary about Archimedes. Despite spending twenty minutes of the hour-long programme drawing a cartoon of said physics teacher on the toilet (he was particularly pleased with the facial expression), eight minutes trying to decide whether he would rather have beriberi or Japanese encephalitis (assuming he had to have one of the two) and fourteen minutes gazing at Jennifer Campbell, some of it had sunk in.

"Good idea. You go grab a pair of skis while I dig a couple of holes under the rock to stick them in."

Within minutes they had managed to squeeze the tail ends of two skis under the right-hand edge of the boat-shaped rock. Using a couple of smaller boulders as their fulcrum, they pushed down on the skis to prise the rock from its position. For a moment it looked like the plan was doomed to failure, as the rock did not move. Ever so slowly, however, the soil relinquished its grip and the rock lifted a few centimetres into the air.

"Quick!" said Angus. "If I hold it up with my ski, you stick a stone in the gap!"

Danny jumped forward and pushed a flat piece of stone into the space between the rock and the ground, to stop it from sinking back. Once he'd done this, Angus released the pressure on his ski. Thankfully, the rock stayed where it was; supported a few inches off the ground on one side.

Kneeling in the snow they peered underneath, Angus flashing the beam of his torch into the darkness. At first, they could see nothing; just a lot of gravel, sand and a few pebbles. For a disheartening moment it appeared that someone else had got there first. Then Danny spotted an unnaturally straight line in the gravel. There was certainly something man-made under there.

Reaching beneath the rock, he tried to pull it out. Whatever it was, it was slippery and he couldn't get a good grip. At last, digging into the sand with his fingers, he found what felt like an oblong piece of metal. He pulled on it. Not the slightest movement. He pulled again; still nothing. Bracing himself against the boulder with his free hand he tugged at it with all his strength. Suddenly it came free and he fell backwards. Almost before he had realised what had happened; he was sitting in the snow, with a startled look on his face and holding a brown rectangular object in his hands. It was tatty, mouldy and incredibly filthy, but it was undoubtedly a briefcase.

CHAPTER TWO

Neither of them said anything for some moments. They had come a long way to find the briefcase, but both of them had secretly doubted that they would. Sixty years was a long time for something to survive under a rock in a harsh sub-arctic environment; there was every chance it could have rotted away completely. Fortunately, the case appeared to be covered with rubberised canvas, which had partially protected it from the damp. Angus finally found his voice.

"Blimey!"

"I'm not sure 'Blimey' really covers it," said Danny. "I think this is more of an occasion for words like…"

"It's in surprisingly good nick," interrupted Angus, picking up the briefcase and examining it up close. "I wonder if the contents are okay?"

"Why not open it up and find out?"

Angus bit his lip, thought for a moment, then shook his head.

"No, this wind is picking up and blowing spindrift around. Also, if the contents have got wet, they might need to be treated very carefully to avoid damaging them. We should wait until we get back to the UK so we can examine them in safe conditions."

Danny was disappointed, but understood the logic. The contents were probably in a very fragile condition. Removing them from the briefcase in anything but ideal conditions would be madness. They would just have to wait a little longer to see what it contained.

★ ★ ★

FIVE DAYS LATER

Danny yawned and stretched himself the full length of the couch. A log fire crackled merrily in the grate as the rain cascaded in tiny writhing rivulets down the living-room window. It had been fun on the Hardangervidda, but he was glad to be home. The journey back to Rjukan across the plateau had been tough; a storm had blown in, bringing high winds and nearly a metre of fresh snow. The days had been long and exhausting, skiing with a heavy pack through the soft snow was the hardest thing Danny had ever done.

The nights had been barely more restful. The wind had torn around their tent, shaking it, thumping it – almost lifting it off the ground. Danny had expected it to disintegrate at any moment, blowing away into the night and leaving them exposed. The tent had survived, however, and they had made it back to Rjukan without succumbing to frostbite or hypothermia.

The briefcase had been put in the airing cupboard the previous night, as soon as they had arrived home from the airport. Angus reckoned it would be dry enough to have an initial look at the contents that evening. Till then, the two of them were spending the day lounging around with all the justification of men who have spent a hard week in the mountains.

A long lie-in had been followed by a lunch of bacon and eggs on toast (four rashers and three eggs each). They had then retreated to the sitting-room where they had watched Raiders of the Lost Ark on DVD and rallied themselves for dinner. Rump steaks (one rare, one medium-rare, topped with fried mushrooms), accompanied by mountains of mashed potato and peas, were swiftly followed by chocolate cheesecake. A short stagger had taken them back to the lounge to lie in food-induced stupefaction, until the dull ache from their over-filled bellies had worn off.

"Right," said Angus, at last. "Let's have a look at this briefcase!"

The airing cupboard seemed to have done the trick: the briefcase appeared to be bone dry. It was still covered in lumps of dried mud, however, and the lock was extremely rusty. Angus had thought of simply breaking the lock with a big screwdriver, but decided against it. He would try to get into the briefcase without damaging it, if possible.

He rummaged through his Raffles Kit — his equipment for getting into places he should really stay out of — after retrieving it from his study.

"A-ha!" he said, pulling out a small canvas roll. "My lock-picks! This should only take a moment."

Once he had squirted a little oil into the corroded mechanism, he set to work. It took him a little longer than he expected — the lock was of high quality — but within a couple of minutes there was a sharp click and the lock sprang.

Easing the case open, they peered inside. It was packed with green cardboard files of varying thickness, each tied with a cotton band. Angus pulled them out one by one and laid them on the coffee table. There were four of them, in varying states of disintegration. The files that had been closest to the ground had suffered most from the damp and were in the poorest condition. On the front cover of each was printed a large black eagle holding a swastika in its claws.

"Might as well start with the one in the best condition," said Angus, pulling forward the file and untying its cotton band. This was the also the largest, being three times as thick as any of the others.

"Wow! Look at this!" he said. Danny leaned in to see better. The documents in this file were in excellent condition and consisted of a variety of technical drawings, sheets of figures and a few faded photographs.

"These are the technical specifications of the V2 rocket!" said Angus. "This would have been red-hot stuff at the time. The V2 was the latest thing in long range weaponry. In fact, the rocket that put the first man on the moon owed its origins to the V2."

"Our German general seems to have had access to some high level stuff," said Danny.

"Undoubtedly. Very few people would have been able to get their hands on this sort of info. I wonder what's in the other files."

The contents of the second file brought a low whistle from Angus's lips. The papers were in poorer condition than those of the first, but there were still plenty of readable pages.

"Blimey. Plans for the Heinkel 162. This guy was really selling the Nazis down the river!"

"What's a Heinkel 162?" asked Danny.

"One of the first ever jet fighter-planes. Fortunately the Nazis were only able to make a few of them before they were defeated. Otherwise the war might have lasted a lot longer than it did."

"Come on, let's open the other files!" said Danny. The excitement was almost unbearable.

"Don't worry, I'm just getting to them!" said Angus, opening the third file. He too was caught up in the moment.

The contents of this file were in much poorer condition; many of the pages were stuck together, having partially dissolved in the damp, and the ink had run into vague grey and blue shadows. Some of the upper pages were readable, however, and looked like they might be progress reports, containing references to sums of Reichsmarks and dates in 1944. All of the documents in this folder had a Nazi eagle and the words 'Mittelbau-Dora' printed across the top.

"What is Mittelbau-Dora?" asked Danny, but this was outwith Angus's knowledge.

"I don't know. My German isn't good enough, I'm afraid. We'll get these documents professionally translated and we'll find out then, I suppose!"

They came at last to the final folder. They did not hold out much hope for it; it looked like a solid lump of papier-mâché. With a little care, however, Angus managed to separate some of the pages. A few blocks of text remained readable, but it amounted to little more than a couple of paragraphs. On the topmost page was a heading. 'Operation Svartalfaheim,' Angus translated. The heading was followed by a few sentences and then a grey blur where there had once been writing. A few more sentences were decipherable on the second and third pages but the rest had been lost to history.

"Well, I'd say that was a pretty good result, overall," said Angus. "There's definitely enough for a story here. I'll get on the phone to the papers tomorrow and see if anyone wants to buy an exclusive. Tell you what, would you like to earn some pocket money?"

"Of course!" said Danny.

"Could you photograph every readable sheet of all these files and save them to the computer? I'll help you set up the tripod and lighting to ensure we get good images of every sheet. Once you've done that, I'll email them to a historian I know who specialises in World War Two. He'll be able to translate them and tell us exactly what's in there."

"Wouldn't it be great if we discovered some incredible secret that nobody knows anything about?" said Danny.

"It would indeed. I'm afraid it's pretty unlikely, though. Most of the really interesting secrets of the Second World War came out a long time ago."

It was past midnight, three days later, when Angus discovered how wrong he was. He had been up late working on his story — *The Times* had agreed to buy an exclusive — and was heading to bed, when the doorbell rang. Puzzled, he made his way to the front door, to see who could be calling at such an unsociable hour. Opening it, he saw two men huddled in the porch, trying to shelter from the wind and rain.

"Good evening, Mr. McKinlay."

The speaker was a striking man in his late thirties.

He had dark eyes that gazed steadily at Angus from under heavy eyebrows and jet-black hair that was combed away from his pale face in thick, wet lines. If it hadn't been for the accent, he would have said the man was Irish. As it was, it was hard to say; he was European certainly, but from where exactly? Angus could not tell.

"May we come in, out of the rain?" It was a reasonable enough question, but there was something about the man that Angus did not like. The hard-faced goon who hovered at the man's shoulder did nothing to dispel his doubts.

"What do you want?"

"We have come to discuss the documents you have found." The man smiled, but there was no friendship in those black eyes.

"I'm sorry, it's late. Come back tomorrow if you like," said Angus, closing the door.

"I'm afraid I cannot wait."

Angus was aware that the door had come to an unexpected stop and glanced down to see what the obstruction was. The man had placed a foot over the threshold, preventing the door from closing. Annoyed, Angus looked up — to find the muzzle of a pistol being held inches from his nose.

"You see, I am in no mood to fool around."

Angus paused. Five years ago he might have frozen, but not now. Now he simply paused.

"Yes, that's clear. Why don't you come in?" He stepped back, gesturing in the direction of the living-room.

"After you," the visitor said. A smile, apparently of genuine amusement this time, flickered briefly on his lips.

"Okay," Angus replied, without returning the smile. "Wipe your feet; you guys look dirty."

They sat in the living-room for more than a minute before the stranger spoke. He sat with his henchman on the couch, under the painting of the Eiger, trying to intimidate Angus with his stare. If Angus hadn't been almost immune to intimidation, it might have worked. The man seemed to fill the room with a malevolent confidence; a vile self-belief that was quite disturbing. Angus paid no heed to the goon; he was an obedient attack-dog, nothing more. His boss (for there was no doubt who was in charge) was something else. Angus sensed in him a fierce intelligence, lethal violence and the barely suppressed energy of the fanatic. This was not a man to underestimate.

"Did you read *The Times* yesterday?" said the man, breaking the silence at last.

"No."

"It does not matter. I have brought it with me." The man reached inside his heavy trench coat and pulled out a folded newspaper. Opening it up, he passed it over to Angus. On page twenty seven was a short paragraph, circled in red.

NAZI SECRETS FOUND BURIED IN NORWEGIAN MOUNTAINS

An amateur archaeologist from Scotland has discovered secret documents dating from World War Two, buried under a rock in the Hardangervidda region of Norway. Among the documents discovered are blueprints for the infamous V2 rocket and an early jet fighter-plane. Mr. Angus McKinlay, from Dunkeld in Perthshire, said: "It's a fascinating find and I am looking forward to having the documents translated and studied by a professional historian."

Angus bit his bottom lip; apart from the bit about being an amateur archaeologist, he couldn't deny any of it. *The Times* must have had a space to fill and decided to whet people's appetites for the main article, which they would be printing on Saturday.

"Who is the professional you are consulting?" asked the man.

"I don't know yet," Angus lied. "I was thinking of calling Dr. Indiana Jones."

"Who is this…Dr. Jones?"

"It was a joke. I haven't decided who to contact yet."

"So nobody else has seen the documents?"

"No."

The man's eyes narrowed as he tried to judge if Angus was telling the truth. He relaxed, apparently satisfied. For a man who didn't play cards, Angus had a great poker face.

"Good. I'm afraid you must hand the briefcase over to me."

"Why?"

"Because I'll kill you if you don't."

"No, I mean, why do you want the briefcase? What could possibly be in there that's worth killing for? And, more to the point, how on earth could you know its contents?"

The man laughed. It was a hoarse, wheezing laugh, straight from the lungs. The laugh of a man with a strange — and probably unpleasant — sense of humour.

"I too am an amateur historian, Mr McKinlay, and I have quite a collection of secret documents myself. I am fully aware of Generalleutnant Weber's treason and how he was killed while trying to escape from Norway. I also have a pretty good idea what secrets he took with him when he deserted. Purely by luck — or perhaps it was destiny — I was in London on business and bought a newspaper... well, I am sure you can guess the rest."

Angus was intrigued; the German's identity was news to him.

"Weber, eh? So who was Generalleutnant Weber?"

The man's face hardened as he realised he had given something away.

"You will have to find that out for yourself. Enough of this nonsense. The briefcase... now!"

Angus was damned if he was going to give this man anything without a fight. He knew it wouldn't be easy; he was outnumbered and his opponents were a tough-looking pair. The goon had a shaved head, square shoulders and the look of a man accustomed to brutality. His superior was more lightly built, but no less fearsome in appearance. Whereas Angus might have fancied his chances against the thug, the boss looked like he could move as fast as Angus and, of course, would have the edge of experience. That was a disadvantage of being one of the good guys: you just didn't get as much opportunity to practise the game of violence.

"What if I say 'no'?"

"Then you will die a long and painful death. Stop wasting my time."

It was then that Angus spotted his chance. Between him and his unwelcome visitors stood a coffee table. He reckoned that if he kicked the table hard enough it would slam painfully into his adversaries' shins; giving himself a vital split second in which to jump up and switch off the light. In the darkness he would escape from the living room, run up the stairs, wake Danny, jump out of the window… and disappear into the night. With any luck they would not be able to break into his safe — where the briefcase was — before he'd had time to summon the police.

Unfortunately, he was not to get the chance to put his plan into practice.

"What's going on?" In the living-room doorway stood a sleepy-eyed youth in blue pyjamas whose mop of dark ginger hair was even more unruly than usual. Yawning, he scratched his bottom and waited for an answer.

"Your father was about to give me a briefcase." The black-eyed villain was grinning from ear to ear. It was clear he had not known about Danny, whose sudden appearance had given him an unexpected tool of persuasion.

"Eh?" said Danny. "Oh, he's not my dad, he's…" He stopped short. He had spotted the pistol in the man's hand.

"Oh."

"Oh, indeed," said the villain, turning to Angus and staring him in the eye. "The briefcase. Now. I am at the limit of my patience."

Angus realised he had lost. If he did not produce the briefcase, Danny would be tortured until he did. He had no doubt that these men were capable of it. Sighing, he got up and went to retrieve it from his safe.

Early the next morning, after an understandably poor night's sleep, Danny and Angus left for Edinburgh to see Professor Clapperton. Clapperton's office was in the William Robertson Building, a layer-cake of glass and concrete that had been shoe-horned into an attractive Georgian square in central Edinburgh some time in the 1960s. They climbed four flights of cheaply-carpeted stairs and walked a long, poorly lit corridor to reach their destination. Angus reached up and thumped on the door.

"Come!"

He turned the handle and they entered.

"Angus! Great to see you! How's it going, mate?" Professor Thomas Clapperton, of Edinburgh University's Centre for the Study of Two World Wars, jumped up from his seat and bounced over. He was a short, wiry man in his early forties, with the dirty-brown tan of a mountaineer and a short crop of tight blond curls on his head. His clothes — which were, quite simply, a symphony in beige — were all made by the same outdoor equipment manufacturer and on his wrist was a comically large watch-cum-altimeter. Everything about him said 'If I wasn't stuck in this god-forsaken office, I would be up the biggest mountain I could find'.

"Hello Tom," said Angus, "Been up any big hills recently?"

"Yes! Just got back from the Alps. Knocked off the Walker Spur at last!"

"Nice one!" Angus was impressed; the Walker Spur on the Grandes Jorasses was one of the classic north face climbs of the Alps and something Tom had been talking about for years.

"But you are not here to talk about that, are you? You are here about this fascinating briefcase!" Clapperton motioned them back to his desk, on which lay copies of the documents that had been so carefully photographed by Danny and then sent by Angus in an email to the professor.

"Yes. Well things have got even more fascinating since I emailed you the documents."

"Really? How so?"

"Because last night some guy and his bullet-headed sidekick waved a gun in my face till I gave them the case."

"You're kidding?" Clapperton's face was a picture of surprise; his eyebrows reaching for his hairline and his jaw for the floor.

"No, completely serious," said Angus, carrying on

to relate the previous night's confrontation. When he had finished, Clapperton let out a whistle.

"Blimey!" he said.

"Yeah, that's what I thought," replied Angus.

"Really?" said Danny, "The word that sprang to my mind was…"

"I wonder why the briefcase was so important to them?" interjected Clapperton, looking keenly at Angus.

"It's a mystery to me. God knows what is in there that is worth murdering someone over. It's more than sixty years since the war ended, you'd think the killing would be over by now!"

Clapperton stroked his chin thoughtfully.

"You know, I've read through all of these documents and nothing leaps out as being particularly sensitive. All the stuff about the V2 rocket and the Heinkel 162 came out years ago. I'm no expert on the Nazi's use of slave labour, but the Mittelberg–Dora information…"

"Yes," said Angus, "we were wondering what Mittelberg–Dora was."

"Mittelberg–Dora was the labour camp where the Nazis kept slave workers who worked at the Mittelwerk factory at Nordhausen. The factory built, among other things, V2 rockets and Heinkel 162s. There is clearly a connection there; perhaps this Generalleutnant Weber was stationed at Nordhausen. In fact, that could go a long way to explaining Weber's defection. It is estimated that around twenty thousand people were worked to death there. No decent man could witness that and do nothing."

"So, do you think that's why those guys came and threatened to kill us if we didn't give them the briefcase?" asked Danny. "That labour camp stuff sounds really nasty, maybe someone who did some evil things is still alive and wants to keep it quiet?"

"That's not a bad theory," said Clapperton, "Except I've been through what little information is in that file and I can't see anything that isn't well known to historians already. It is mostly invoices for construction materials and requests for more slave-labourers to be sent from other concentration camps. Pretty unpleasant stuff, but like I say, well documented and relatively common knowledge."

"So what on earth did they want?" Angus sounded more than a little exasperated.

"I'm afraid all I can think is that they were after whatever was in the fourth file," said Clapperton. "I can't see what good it would do them, though;

it was in terrible condition. Most of what is left is broken fragments of text which make no sense on their own. All I can tell is that the file contained the details of something called Operation Svartalfaheim and a reference to…"

Clapperton paused and looked down at a notebook on his desk.

"… The Hood of Death" he muttered.

"The what?" said Danny.

"That's what it translates as – 'The Hood of Death', as in the cowl that the grim reaper wears to hide his naked skull."

"Cheery lot those Nazis, weren't they?"

"Oh, there is also a reference to Schneibstein, a mountain in the Bavarian Alps, near the town of Berchtesgaden. Of course, Berchtesgaden is famous for being the location of Hitler's mountain retreat, but I've never heard of Operation Svartalfaheim and God only knows what the Hood of Death is."

"What does the word 'Svartalfaheim' mean?" asked Angus. "Might there be a clue in the name of the operation?"

"Good question," replied Clapperton. "While the British chose the names of their operations randomly, the Nazis often chose a name which hinted at the nature of the operation itself. A bit daft when you think about it. If you give me a minute I will ask Herr Google what 'Svartalfaheim' means."

Clapperton crashed into the chair behind his desk, clicked his mouse a couple of times and thumped out 'Svartalfaheim' on the keyboard.

"Hmm," he said, after a brief moment. "It's actually a Norwegian word. It is the underground realm of the dark elves of Norse mythology. Oh well. You live and learn."

"Yeah. Though not much in this case," said Angus, clearly unimpressed by the revelation.

There was silence for a moment as the three of them were lost in thought. Then Angus clapped his hands together and smiled. He had clearly come to a decision.

"Well, I don't think there's much more we can learn by sitting on our butts in Scotland."

Danny knew his uncle well enough to know exactly what he was thinking.

"Let me guess," he said. "We are off to the Bavarian Alps."

CHAPTER THREE

Danny had assumed they would fly to the Bavarian Alps, like they had to Norway, but Angus had decided they should go overland. After all, he argued, they did not know what might happen or where they might need to go after Bavaria, so it would be better to have their own transport.

Angus's faithful old Toyota Hi-Lux had had a thorough overhaul since the beating it had taken in the Sahara. The damaged bonnet, front wing, front bumper and driver's door had been replaced and the engine, gear box and clutch had all been stripped down and serviced. Most importantly of all, the heater had been fixed — Danny no longer had to wear gloves and a woolly hat on long winter journeys.

It took them three days to reach Berchtesgaden from Dunkeld. With little else to do, Danny watched – to the droning soundtrack of the Toyota's engine – the endless, hypnotic procession of the landscape. It was strangely fascinating to see the gradual metamorphosis of a continent. On the first day they passed through the familiar rolling pasture, hedgerows, and church spires of England. On the second day came the wide plains, yellow fields and empty, tree-lined roads of France. On the third day, as they hammered along the autobahn, he saw the rugged hills and dark forests of Germany slowly grow into mountains. At last, in early-afternoon sunshine, they reached the Alps.

The last few miles to Berchtesgaden, after leaving the autobahn, were a slow climb up a long winding road between high peaks still plastered with the winter's snow, and as they drove higher the air became sharp with the cold. Danny cranked up the heater and warmed his hands over the vents. Above them, despite the cold, the sky was deep blue and the sun glared brightly off the snow-clad mountains.

Shielding his eyes with his hand, Danny peered at the country around him. It was picture-postcard beautiful; almost too pretty. There was something sterile about the green meadows and whitewashed chalets that was at odds with his experience of the countryside. There were no broken-down tractors slowly disintegrating into the earth or overgrown outbuildings scattered with rusting machinery. Danny looked curiously at a pristine field artfully arranged with brown and white cows. Was he imagining it? In a field of about thirty cows, he couldn't see a single cowpat.

They soon found what they were looking for; a house displaying the word 'Zimmer' on a sign in a window. A bustling old lady welcomed them into her home and ushered them into a room with a "Ja? Is gut, ja?" It *was* good: it was spacious, had comfy beds, a TV and an en suite bathroom. It even had a small balcony with a view of the mountains. Angus handed over some Euros and they had their home for the next couple of days.

Stretching himself out on the bed nearest the balcony, Danny sighed with satisfaction.

"Don't get me wrong, I do like travelling, but sometimes it's great to get where you are going!"

Angus laughed and crashed down on his bed like a ton of wet cement.

"Yeah, I know what you mean!"

They lay in silence for a while, thinking about the last couple of days driving across Europe. The smells of busy roads and of the countryside in the spring, the moments of sunshine and the sudden torrential cloudbursts, the distant towns and the looming mountains. Europe — slowly changing as it passed beneath their wheels. Eventually, Angus spoke up.

"Right, I'm starving. Let's go and find something to eat before I fall asleep in my clothes."

The next morning the sky was still blue, with just a few curls of high altitude cirrus clouds on the western horizon. This was good news, as that day they planned to climb Schneibstein, the mountain mentioned in the fourth file. Danny was extremely excited. He had climbed quite a few small mountains in the Lake District and the Pennines with his father, and Angus had taken him up a couple of slightly larger ones in the Cairngorms; but, at 2276 metres, Schneibstein was significantly higher than any mountain Danny had ever climbed. Moreover – this would be his first Alpine summit.

Climbing Schneibstein wasn't, as Angus admitted, a very scientific approach, but he couldn't think of anything better. Their only concrete lead was the fact the mountain was mentioned in the fourth file. He hoped that a close inspection of the mountain would give them some hint as to what Operation Svartalfaheim had involved or what the Hood of

Death might have been. Perhaps some forgotten relic of the war would provide the next clue. If they were very lucky, some tiny shred of evidence might remain to suggest why people were prepared to kill to get their hands on Weber's briefcase.

Studying their map, they realised that the easiest way to get onto Schneibstein would be to take the skiers' cable car to the top of a nearby mountain named Jenner. A relatively short hike to the east would take them to Schneibstein's north ridge, along which they would climb to reach the summit.

The Jennerbahn cable car whisked them quickly up to the top of Jenner at 1800 metres, and they were soon hiking past skiers and snowboarders. The sun seemed even more glaring up here and Angus put on his sunglasses. Turning to Danny he gave them a tap them with his forefinger.

"Put on your sunnies, mate. All the snow and sunshine at this altitude... you'll go snow-blind in no time."

"Oh, right..." Danny pulled out his sunglasses and put them on.

"Sun cream too," said Angus, passing over a bright yellow tube of factor 50. "A few years ago I went climbing in the French alps with a guy who didn't use any sun cream. His lips got so badly burnt he couldn't eat solids for a fortnight — lived off milk, lukewarm soup and orange juice. Looked like he'd been chewing a razor blade."

"Jeez, I love your gruesome stories of adventure, Angus."

"Just making the point…"

"Yes. Sun cream is important. Thanks."

After an hour or so they had left the confines of the ski resort behind and had reached the mountain hut at the foot of the north ridge of Schneibstein. Pausing here for a short rest they gazed around at their environment. Everything was still caked in the winter's snow, except for the gnarled and stunted pine trees that scattered the mountain side — the spring sunshine had already melted the snow from their dark green branches.

The ridge they stood on was, in fact, an international border. To their west, where they had come from, stood Germany and Berchtesgaden. To their east, between high, threatening cliffs, a steep valley plummeted down into Austria. Far below, they could see sunlit pasture and cosy alpine lodges; but they seemed like a very long way away indeed.

Turning south-southeast, they began their climb to the summit of Schneibstein. A narrow path had been trodden into the old snow by previous mountaineers and the going was relatively easy. Above, the sky remained mostly blue, although the few white curls of cirrus in the west had developed into a ragged silver blanket.

"Hmm." Angus paused briefly to peer up at the clouds. "We'll need to keep an eye on that. Could mean a change for the worse is on its way."

"Really? Might we have to turn back?" asked Danny. While he didn't much like the idea of being caught high on a mountainside in bad weather, he was much more concerned that he might not get the chance to bag his first alpine peak.

"I don't think we need to worry about that just yet," replied Angus. "Worth keeping an eye on the sky, though. Just in case."

They continued steadily upwards, their boots crunching rhythmically in the snow. Occasionally they would lift their eyes to gaze around at the beautiful and majestic mountains that crowded together in this isolated corner of the Alps. Sometimes they stared upwards, peering at the clouds, trying to gauge what might be happening with the weather. Mostly though, they looked downwards, picking their footsteps on the icy trail.

At a little under 2000 metres, the going suddenly got much tougher. The mountain rose in front of them in a steep bank of snow, up which the trail continued in short zigzags. They had to use their ice-axes here, driving their shafts into the snow to ensure they kept their balance on the vertigo-inducing slope. About half-way up this steep section, Danny paused and looked over his shoulder at the mountainside below and felt a shiver that was nothing to do with the cold. Below him the mountain swept away into Austria in a long steep slope. He knew that if he lost his footing here he would fall hundreds of metres.

Trying to dismiss the thought from his mind, he climbed as fast as he dared after Angus, being very careful to thrust his ice-axe deep into the snow with every step. Angus was at the top of the steep section now, reaching over the lip of a small cornice and plunging the pick of his ice-axe into the snow beyond. He was silhouetted by the dazzling sun that hung high in the sky above. Danny could see tiny particles of ice blowing over the cornice and around Angus's head, sparkling like microscopic diamonds in the glare.

He watched as Angus pulled himself up, threw a leg over the overhang of wind-blown snow and then disappeared. In seconds he was there himself, poking his head over the lip to see what lay beyond. As soon as he did so, however, a sudden gust of wind blasted him with spindrift. With his face burning from the freezing wind and the ice melting on his skin, he squinted upwards to where Angus was standing. His uncle was looking up towards the summit, his back to the wind, calmly waiting for Danny to catch up.

Danny looked back again, down the precipitous mountain-side, and immediately wished he hadn't. If he slipped, there was nothing to stop him falling to a grisly death. He had a sudden, grim vision of his own corpse lying at the foot of the mountain, arms and legs twisted at unnatural angles, a splash of crimson on a white background...

"Come on, mate. We haven't got all day!" Angus shouted above the wind. He seemed completely unmoved by the precariousness of their position. He didn't seem to have any concept of his own mortality. More importantly, he didn't seem to have any concept of Danny's.

"Okay, but it's a big drop if I mess up! I'm not sure…"

"What?" The wind was making it difficult for them to hear each other.

"I said: it's a long drop if I mess up! I'm not sure I can do it!" Danny yelled.

"I can't hear you!" Angus yelled back. The wind was ripping the words from their lips and casting them into oblivion.

"I SAID… ONE SLIP AND I'M STRAWBERRY JAM!"

"WHAT?"

"OH… FORGET IT!"

Danny took a deep breath and plunged the pick of his ice-axe into the snow behind the cornice, in the way he had seen Angus do. It made a satisfying 'thunk' as it bit into the snow and, making sure of his balance, he gave it an experimental tug. To his relief the snow seemed to be quite firm and he thought it should take his weight as he pulled himself up. Wasting no more time thinking about the consequences of a fall, he heaved hard on the axe while swinging his right leg up over the cornice. "Pull... come on, pull!" he growled at himself as he fought to drag his body onto the level ground beyond. Moments later he was there, lying flat out and panting with the effort.

"Well done, pal!" He heard Angus shout above the wind. "What was all that yelling about jam?"

Danny sighed. "It doesn't matter."

"The lunchtime sandwiches are cheese and salami, if that's what you were wondering."

"No. I had rather more important things on my mind."

"Well, the deep and meaningful contemplation can wait. We've got a mountain to climb and this wind is getting a wee bit brisk for my liking. The sooner we are up and down the better. First things first, though. It's pretty icy up here. We'd better put on our crampons."

Pulling the nylon bags containing their crampons from their packs they set them down in the snow and started to strap the steel spikes to their boots. It was a fiddly job that meant they had to take off their gloves and Danny's fingers were soon stinging from the freezing wind and from contact with snow and cold metal. In a few minutes, however, they had securely fastened the crampons to their feet and were climbing the icy slope to the summit.

From this point upwards, there was no longer a trail to follow. Either the mountaineers who had left the trail below the cornice had turned back, or the snow was simply too hard to show their footprints. The snow up here had frozen into a solid layer of white ice and, save for the tiny holes made by the points of their crampons, neither Danny nor Angus left any mark of their passing.

At last, in the early afternoon, they took the final few steps to the top of Schneibstein. The summit was a broad, windswept plateau surrounded by a spectacular panorama of soaring peaks. Huge alpine mountains encircled them like the ragged jaws of a prehistoric beast. Above them, despite the thickening clouds to the west, the sky was still blue and the sun still shone with aggressive brilliance. The wind, with nothing to check its progress, tore powerfully over the summit, making them lurch and stagger like Hogmanay drunks.

Underneath his balaclava Danny was grinning like the Cheshire cat. This was it; his first Alpine summit, and it was everything he had hoped it would be. Everything about the day — the sun, the wind, the biting cold, the incredible panorama of snow-clad peaks, even that moment of bowel-clenching terror as he had climbed the cornice — it was all completely and utterly perfect. He knew he would remember this day for the rest of his life.

After a few minutes, they turned back in the direction they had come and began to descend. It was too cold on the summit to stop and have lunch, so they retreated a short distance to where a large boulder offered the promise of shelter. Out of the wind it was much more comfortable; there was even the slightest suggestion of warmth from the sun. Angus produced a plastic lunch box and tossed it to Danny.

"Cheese and Salami sandwiches!" he said, and grinned.

"Thanks," said Danny, popping open the lunchbox. However cavalier Angus might be with their lives, he did make a damn fine sandwich. Today's was crusty bread, emmental cheese, salami, lettuce and tomato, with a dollop of mayonnaise and a soupcon of wholegrain mustard. Wrestling with an ambitiously-sized mouthful of damn fine sandwich, Danny nudged his uncle to get his attention.

"Fo, any ideaf what Operation Fartalfaheim might be? Or the 'Hood of Death'?"

The corners of Angus's mouth turned down a little.

"No, not really. I haven't seen anything that suggests the Nazis were up to anything on the mountain, have you?"

"Nothing."

"I have been thinking about that name though; 'Operation Svartalfaheim'. Do you remember? Tom told us that 'Svartalfaheim' meant the underground realm of the dark elves in Norse mythology."

"Yes."

"Well, have a look at this rock." Angus slapped their stony windbreak with the palm of his hand. "What kind of rock do you think that is?"

"I have no idea," Danny admitted.

"It's limestone. This whole landscape is made of the stuff. And limestone landscapes are famous for one particular type of geological feature."

"What?"

Angus grinned.

"Caves!"

"Caves?"

"Caves!"

"Of course! Caves!" Danny shook his head in

disbelief at his own stupidity. "It's obvious when you think about it!"

"Well, it's not that obvious," said Angus. "In fact, I think connecting the two requires a remarkable talent for lateral thinking..."

"So, rather than looking around up here on the mountain top, we should be looking down there..." Danny gestured towards the valley, "...for caves, or mines maybe?" He was gripped by a sudden excitement. Seconds ago he would have been happy to spend hours huddled behind their rock, eating his lunch and admiring the view. Now he was itching to get going, to head down into the valley and hunt for caves.

"Well, I suppose they could be anywhere," said Angus who, although he might not have admitted it, was also feeling a little excited. "But I suspect the most likely location is somewhere on Schneibstein. After all, it is mentioned in the file. Caves don't need to be in the bottoms of valleys or at the feet of cliffs. I've seen a cave entrance higher than 2000 metres up in the Julian Alps. Wait a minute..." Angus reached into his pack and, after a moment of rummaging, pulled out a pair of binoculars. Flicking off the lens covers he raised them to his eyes and started to sweep the mountainside for any sign of a cave entrance.

His search was fruitless, however. From their position near the summit, they could actually see very little of the mountain. After a minute or two he passed the binoculars to Danny, who also failed to find any suggestion of a cave.

"We really need to get off the mountain and look at it from below," said Angus. "Preferably from as many angles as possible. We will probably need to drive over into Austria to look at it from there too."

Without delay, they shouldered their packs and set off down the mountain to catch the Jennerbahn cable-car. As they went, they kept their eyes peeled for anything that might be the entrance to a cave.

Descending the cornice was not as bad as Danny had worried it might be. Partly because Angus went first and Danny thought that there was a chance his uncle could catch him if he fell, but mostly because he had already conquered his fear. Having climbed up it without falling off, he saw no reason why he should not descend it equally safely.

As they got lower, the conditions became less fierce and before long they could walk normally, without leaning far into the wind or staggering in the sudden gusts. Approaching the foot of the ridge Danny looked again down the dark, steep-sided valley that led into Austria. To his right the valley sides were steep and covered with dark conifer trees, to his left they were even steeper. Grey cliffs, too sheer for the snow to lie upon, soared above the lumpen crags and vast boulders in the valley bottom.

It was as he stared at this breath-taking scene that he spotted a feature that had escaped his notice on the way up. It was a curious overhang at the top of a crag a short way down the valley. It was unusually shaped; certainly he had never seen anything quite like it before. It looked very much like…

"ANGUS!" he yelled. His uncle was already a hundred metres ahead. He began racing after him, running as fast as he could over the icy trail.

"ANGUS!" he yelled again and this time the shout was heard. Angus stopped and turned.

"Look!" Danny said, as he reached the point where Angus stood. "Look at that overhang!"

"What overhang?"

"That one! Down there…

"Oh, wait a minute… yes, I see it."

"What do you think it looks like?"

"It looks like an overhang."

Danny sighed. Angus peered more carefully at the

overhang, sudden realisation showing in the curl of his lips.

"Now do you see it?" said Danny.

The rock above the overhang was pointed at the top and came forward in a rounded protrusion that curled downwards at the sides, like the hood on a boxer's robe or monk's habit. Underneath the overhang the rock was smooth, but an imaginative soul might have seen the suggestion of a gaunt face in the various shades of grey.

"It does resemble the headgear of the grim reaper, doesn't it?" Angus said.

"You think that could be it? You think that's the 'hood of death'?"

"Could be. Only one way to find out: let's go and take a look."

The overhang was no more than a few hundred metres away and they turned off the track, heading straight towards it through the virgin snow. Fifty metres from their destination, Angus stopped suddenly.

"What is it?" asked Danny, recognising in his uncle's body language that something had caught his attention. Angus said nothing. Turning to look at Danny he simply raised an eyebrow and pointed at the snow ahead of them.

About ten metres away, there were footprints. The trail came up the valley from Austria and headed straight for the overhang. Striding over, Angus bent to examine the footprints more closely.

"Two... no... three men have come this way. Reasonably recently, I'd guess. Perhaps yesterday or the day before."

They hurried on, wondering who would come to such a strange part of the mountainside, but suspecting that they knew the answer. The direction they were heading in did not lead anywhere other than the overhang. It was well away from any of the routes a person would take if they were heading between Germany and Austria, or climbing one of the nearby mountains.

The footprints continued towards a jutting shoulder of rock at the foot of the cliff, deep in the shadow of the 'hood'. As they closed in, they saw a great confusion of footprints in the snow, as though someone had been searching the cliff face for something. The swathe of trampled snow extended to the far side of the shoulder and they followed it round, to see if anything lay hidden on the other side. What they saw left them both speechless for some moments. Eventually, Danny broke the silence.

"Cor…"

Angus eyed him questioningly.

"Blimey?" he asked.

Danny was still staring ahead, his eyes wide and his jaw slack.

"Yes," he said. "I think that is the word I was looking for."

CHAPTER FOUR

Before them, clearly cut into the rock by the hand of man, was an opening; a dark doorway leading straight into the mountainside. It was about two metres high, but narrow, being less than a metre wide. On the ground lay the shattered remnants of a door — thick planks and a rusting iron frame. Angus bent to examine the debris.

"Looks like it's been broken down quite recently," he said. "The splinters haven't had time to discolour in the sun. My guess is that whoever left the footprints also smashed open the door. He lifted up a piece of planking. "The door was painted the same colour as the rock. From further than a few metres away, you'd never have known it was here."

Danny peered into the dark tunnel that lay beyond the doorway, but could see nothing in its Stygian interior. He knew that if they wanted to unravel the mystery surrounding Weber's briefcase they would have to go inside and have a look around. The thought made him uncomfortable; he didn't really like dark, enclosed spaces. Ever since the Sons of Rissouli had tied him up and put a bag over his head, he had suffered from claustrophobia.

He was tempted to suggest that Angus should explore the tunnel on his own. The doorway was dark and menacing, but there was also something undeniably intriguing and mysterious about it. He suspected that if he did not go inside he would regret it.

"Shall we take a look then?" he said, throwing off his pack so that he could get to the head-torch inside.

"I think it would be rude not to!" said Angus, who was grinning like the cat who'd got the cream.

There is no light quite so bright as the sunlight on a snow-covered mountain and no darkness quite so complete as the darkness inside a cave. Even with the benefit of torches, it took them a few moments to become accustomed to the gloom.

A few paces down the tunnel, they realised that only the doorway was man-made. Further in, the tunnel widened into a natural fissure that descended rapidly towards the heart of the mountain.

Danny bit his lip and tried not to think about the

millions of tons of rock above their heads, or about the fact that no-one knew where they were. He tried not to think what would happen if a rock-fall closed the tunnel behind them or if they got lost in the darkness — or if the batteries in their torches went flat. He tried, but it was difficult. The darkness was so complete, the shadows so overwhelmingly black and the tunnel so small and cramped, that it was hard not to think sinister thoughts.

Underfoot the ground was a smooth, undulating layer of hard clay. The rock that surrounded them was sometimes rough, sometimes rippled and sometimes as smooth as glass. It was mostly dull grey in colour, although the occasional rust-red band could be seen amongst the strata. The air, oddly, seemed warmer than it had done on the surface and there was a slight feeling of dampness that suggested the temperature was above freezing.

Before long, the tunnel began to level off and open out. At its entrance, the tunnel was only a few centimetres wider than their shoulders and they could have easily touched the rock above their heads with an outstretched hand. Now it was ten metres high and getting wider with every step.

Soon the tunnel widened into a cave. It was just

how Danny imagined a cave would look. There were long, thin stalactites hanging from the roof and below them, dumpy, malformed stalagmites rising from the floor. Black shadows scattered the uneven walls; shadows that might conceal nothing more than a hollow in the limestone bedrock — or the entrance to a whole new catacomb.

Scattered between the stalagmites were muddy puddles, and at the far end of the cave was a deep pool of black water. As they looked around, their torches swung long beams through the air like the searchlights in a war film. The ragged array of stalactites and stalagmites threw serrated shadows against the cave walls which seemed to flicker and sway as the torchlight passed over them.

It was, thought Danny, like playing some horribly atmospheric computer game set in the underground lair of a ferocious beast. All he could see was what lay directly in front of his torch, very much like the narrow view on a TV screen. The darkness to either side of that narrow beam of light was a mystery until he turned and pointed his torch in that direction. Anything at all could approach them while they were simply looking the other way. Who could tell what horrors lurked in the unlit blackness, in the deep shadows beyond the next formation of rock or, in the darkest place of all…the space behind his back?

"Stop being stupid!" he said to himself, unaware that the words had left his mouth.

"Eh?" said Angus. "Who's being stupid?"

"Oh sorry. I was just thinking aloud."

Angus looked thoughtful.

"I suppose it is a bit stupid when you think about it," he said. "Charging about without proper caving equipment or a map of the cave system. If there was a collapse in the entrance tunnel we'd never find our way out… and it's not as if anyone even knows that we are down here."

"That's not what I meant. I meant I was being stupid for imagining monsters in the dark, but thank you for reminding me of the real dangers."

"And, of course," Angus continued, "If we do run into those thugs again, this would be the perfect place to do us in."

"I hadn't thought of that. Thanks very much."

"Shoot us in the back and throw us in that pool," said Angus cheerfully, pointing at a stretch of dark water at the far end of the cave. "No-one would ever find our bodies."

"You're not helping."

There was silence for a moment as Angus studied Danny's face.

"You don't look very happy," he said. "Do you want to go back to the surface?"

"No," Danny decided. "We've come this far, let's get it over with."

They picked their way forward, through the muddy puddles and misshapen stalagmites, searching for the reason why someone had covered the entrance to the cave with a heavy, camouflaged door. There had to be something down there more interesting than geological formations. They found nothing, however, and soon reached the edge of the dark pool of water that marked the furthermost boundary of the cave. There remained only one place still to be explored. On the other side of the pool, about thirty metres away, lay a dark void in the rock

"How deep do you think the pool is?" asked Danny, knowing that they would have to try to cross it. They would never be able to leave the cave without finding out what lay in that intriguing area of shadow.

"It doesn't look too deep," said Angus, shining his torch down into the water. It was amazingly clear, like the water in a mountain stream. It appeared to be about 70 centimetres deep. Angus pulled off his boots and socks, followed by his trousers.

"I'm going to see if we can wade across. Wait here."

Leaving his discarded clothing and rucksack with Danny he waded swiftly into the water and began making for the other side. Danny could tell by the stiff-legged, hurried manner in which he walked that the water was extremely cold. He was almost at the far side when the water suddenly got a little deeper, rising from his thighs to around his waist. Angus had to pull his thermal vest, fleece and jacket up around his armpits to keep them dry. Finally he reached the far side of the pool and turned around.

"Come on in! The water's lovely!" he shouted, the final word echoing eerily around the cave.

"It looks freezing!" Danny shouted back, the echo of his words emphasising the coldness of the water. "… freezing… freezing… freezing…"

"No, it's actually surprisingly warm… warm… warm…"

Danny shrugged and pulled off his own boots, socks and trousers and waded quickly into the pool. He had been right. It was absolutely, unbelievably, heart-stoppingly freezing. It was more than just cold, it was painful. So cold he heard his voice go up an octave as he yelled across at his uncle.

"Warm! My butt! ...butt! ...butt!"

By the time he reached the other side, Angus had pulled himself up into the dark void and was peering into it with the help of his head-torch.

"Anything in there?" Danny asked, climbing up next to his uncle.

"Yes indeed," said Angus quietly.

Before them was a small room. It wasn't simply a cave or hollow, it was definitely a room, having been cut straight and square from the bedrock. It wasn't terribly big, just four metres by four metres, and had been fitted with shelves. On the shelves lay some packing cases — all of which had been broken open. Of their contents, there was no sign.

The packing cases were old and the nails that held them together had gone rusty. Angus lifted one up to examine it. It was a curious shape; over a metre tall and nearly as wide, but only 30 centimetres or so deep. Danny picked up another of exactly the same proportions. There were six of these crates, all roughly the same size, and one smaller crate about a third of the size of the others.

"What do you think was in these?" asked Danny.

"No idea," replied Angus. "But whatever it was someone clearly thought it was worth going to all the effort of hiding it down here."

"So this is what we came down here for? A pile of bloomin' firewood? What a waste of time!" Danny said, the disappointment etched deeply into his voice. There was silence for a moment as they regarded the empty crates despondently. Then Angus dropped suddenly to his knees. A second later he rose, holding something carefully in the palm of his hand.

"A waste of time?" he said with a smile, holding the object out for Danny to inspect. It was a small paper packet with the word 'Drina' written across it in red.

"A cigarette packet? Woo-hoo." Danny sounded singularly unimpressed.

Angus laughed.

"Well, it may not look like much, but it might tell us who took the contents of these crates." He looked at his watch. "We had better get going, we'll have to hurry if we are to catch the last cable car off Jenner."

Back at the guest house Angus borrowed a roll of sticky tape, a pencil and a few sheets of white paper from their puzzled landlady. Returning to their room he set out these items on a bedside table along with his Swiss Army knife and the cigarette packet. Picking up the knife he examined it for a moment before pulling open one of the blades.

"Nail file!" he said, grinning at Danny. "And I thought this was the one blade I'd never use!"

Taking up the pencil, he began rubbing its point along the file above one of the sheets of paper. Before long, a tiny pile of graphite had appeared on the piece of paper. Once the pencil became blunt, he used the penknife's normal cutting blade to sharpen it and then began filing down the point again. After a few minutes, he had a nice little mound of black graphite dust.

Placing the cigarette packet on another sheet of white paper, he then sprinkled the graphite dust over it. Turning the packet over he sprinkled it again, repeating his actions until the whole packet was covered with a fine coating of black powder. Then, very carefully, he bent down and blew the excess graphite dust away. Using a pair of tweezers from his first aid kit, he picked it up and held it under the bedside lamp. Peering at it closely, they could see a mass of tiny black lines smeared across its surface.

"Are you looking for finger prints?" asked Danny, although he fancied he already knew the answer.

"Yes. Hmm…" Angus was silent for a moment. The packet was covered in prints — his makeshift graphite fingerprint powder was showing them up admirably — unfortunately, they were also badly smeared and lay one on top of another. On the bottom of the pack, however, he found what he was looking for — a clear print which had not been overlaid by any others.

"Bingo!"

Cutting a piece of sticky tape from the roll, he smoothed it down over the print. When he pulled the tape away, the black swirls of the print came with it. Being very careful not to get his own fingerprints on the tape, he pressed it down on a clean sheet of paper and showed it to Danny. Even without a magnifying glass Danny could clearly see the lines and swirls of the black finger print against the white of the paper. Angus laughed and rubbed his hands together with obvious delight.

"Danny, pass me my phone will you?"

Switching it on to speaker-phone he dialled a number and placed it on the table between them. It hummed a few times, there was a click and the sound of someone clearing their throat.

"Chief Inspector Newby," a gruff voice barked — the voice of a man up to his eyeballs in work, dammit.

"Hello Newby, Angus here. Danny too."

"Ah! Hello chaps!" The voice had mellowed immediately. "How are you fellows?"

"Pretty good, thanks. You?"

"Work is pretty hectic at the moment, but mostly on the oojah side of spiff, old chap."

Danny looked at his uncle quizzically. Sometimes it seemed like the old policeman was talking a foreign language. Angus gave him the thumbs up to indicate that Newby had meant he was in good form.

"I won't keep you long if you are busy. We are in Germany looking into a story. I have a favour to ask if that's okay?"

"No problem, I figure Special Branch owes you a couple of favours."

"Great! If I email you a photograph of a fingerprint, do you think you could run it through the INTERPOL files for me?"

"Certainly, it doesn't take long. When do you need the results?"

"Can you get back to me by tomorrow morning?

Things are moving pretty fast here…"

"Say no more about it old chap, send it over and I'll get on to it right away."

"Thanks Newby, see you soon."

Ending the call, Angus turned and smiled at Danny.

"If the guy who smoked these cigarettes has a criminal record, then his prints will be somewhere on the INTERPOL files, and we'll know exactly who we are dealing with."

"But what if he doesn't have a criminal record?" asked Danny. "We won't have any other leads to follow."

Angus grinned widely.

"Call me a hopeless old optimist, Danny, but I'm guessing that won't be an issue!"

The next morning there was a new email in Angus's inbox, not from Chief Inspector Newby, but from Professor Clapperton at Edinburgh University. Angus opened it curiously. After a couple of minutes he glanced across at Danny, who was lying on his bed doing his best to digest a gargantuan German breakfast.

"Listen to this. Tom has done a bit of research on Weber's career. Apparently, for most of the war Weber worked on Hermann Goering's personal staff."

"Who was Hermann Goering?"

"One of Hitler's pals. Head of the German Air Force if I remember right. Anyway, Weber worked on Goering's staff, procuring art for his collection. The Nazis did that, they pinched art from every country they invaded and the top men — Hitler, Goering, Goebbels and the like — shared it amongst themselves as the spoils of war.

"In July 1944, Weber was posted to the labour camp at Nordhausen, which is presumably where he saw the Nazis for what they really were and decided to defect."

"Must have been a bit of a shock," said Danny, "working with old paintings to working in a slave labour camp."

"Aye."

Danny looked thoughtful for a moment.

"What happened to the art at the end of the war? Did the original owners get their art back?"

"Those that were still alive, I suppose. When the Nazis realised they were going to lose, they tried to hide a lot of the art they'd stolen, or even to smuggle it out of Europe. Presumably so they could sell it after the war. Some of it is still missing, I believe."

"What sort of places did they hide it in?" asked Danny. There was a twinkle in his eye, a twinkle very much like the one Angus would get when a realisation struck him.

"All sorts of places. Salt mines were a particular favourite I believe, something to do with the atmosphere being ideal... for... storing..."

"There were paintings in those crates!" They said in unison, grinning happily at one another.

"Of course!" cried Angus. "Art plundered by the Nazis! That was what made Weber's files so valuable! The men who stole the briefcase from us knew it might contain clues to the location of art stolen by the Nazis and hidden in the mountains!"

"I wonder who they were?" said Danny "I wonder how they knew about Weber and the art?"

At that very moment, as if in answer to his question, Angus's laptop made a doink, doink noise to signal that he had received another email. It was from Newby.

Red, White & Black

Hello chaps,

Good to hear from you yesterday. Hope you are both well and not being shot at (anything is possible with you pair).

Am intrigued by this fingerprint. Damn intrigued. Where on earth did you find it? The INTERPOL database of fingerprints says it belongs to a thoroughly despicable thug who goes by the name of Nikola Maric. Not much is known about him, I'm afraid. It's not even known if Nikola Maric is his real name, though I'd wager Tomatin to turps that it isn't. Some people suspect he is ex-Serbian special forces — he appeared out of nowhere just after the Yugoslavian War ended in 2001. He's been linked to various violent robberies and a couple of serious frauds, but nothing has ever been proved against him.

INTERPOL also suspect him to be the new head of an international Neo-Nazi group called The Adler Kommando who are a shower of bullies, cowards, thugs and criminals who fancy themselves as the master race. They are responsible for some very nasty attacks on all sorts of minorities; Jews, blacks, gays, even disabled people. They started with political rallies. You know the kind of thing — a few shaven-headed thugs shouting their heads off to anyone who will listen. When no-one paid much attention, they moved up to petty thuggery — beating people up in the street and so on. Recently, however, they have become considerably more professional — and graduated to terrorism. It may be that Maric's leadership has caused this move to the big leagues.

You will remember the nail bomb that was exploded in an Algerian café in Paris last year. That was the Adler Kommando. No hard evidence has been found against Maric, or the French would have locked him up long ago, but INTERPOL are pretty sure he's their man.

I have attached an electronic copy of Maric's INTERPOL file to this email.

It doesn't contain an awful lot I'm afraid, but there is a mug-shot of him and the address of a house he owns in Chamonix in the French Alps.

Take care, boys. Maric is a clever and dangerous man.

Angus looked at Danny and whistled.

"I think we might have stumbled on something big," he said. "Guys like that don't bother themselves with chicken feed."

"You're not kidding," said Danny quietly; he was more than a little worried by what he'd read. Should they really be getting mixed up with men like these? He'd barely survived his last brush with murderous criminals; maybe he wouldn't be so lucky this time.

"Let's have a look at this Maric character and see what we are up against," said Angus, clicking on the file that Newby had attached to his email. Scrolling down past the first page of text, he came to the mug-shot of Maric — and stared into a face they knew all too well. It was the face of the man who had visited them on that cold, rain-lashed night in Dunkeld. The man with the dark hair, the white face and the empty, black eyes of a killer.

CHAPTER FIVE

Danny had been impressed by the mountains around Berchtesgaden, but Chamonix was something else again. The town was squeezed into a narrow valley between dizzyingly steep peaks that rose in serrated blades against the alpine sky. As they drove slowly down the main street in the hunt for their hotel, he craned his neck and stared in wonder at the murderous-looking mountains looming over the shops and hotels.

He knew that Angus had spent six months skiing and climbing here when he was younger; in his own words 'not doing anything very productive, just having a helluva lot of fun!'

"You'll have climbed some of these peaks then?" he asked.

"Yep."

He pointed to a huge white dome that dominated the valley.

"How about that one?"

"That's Mont Blanc. I did it from the other side."

"Cool. What about those?" He indicated a ragged

row of needle-like spires to their left.

"Aiguille du Plan. Yes. Not as difficult as they look."

"Blimey." He wondered how difficult that was; they looked like extremely tough climbs to him.

Chamonix, thought Danny, knew its place in the world. Towering above it were the most spectacular mountains in Europe and it was doing everything it could to exploit that. The place was crammed with climbing and skiing shops, restaurants, bars, hotels and backpackers' hostels. Every inch of it was dedicated to servicing the needs of the vast number of tourists who came from all over the world to hike, climb, ski, snowboard, parapente, base-jump, mountain-bike or simply to stand and stare. Maybe that was why Maric chose to live here; one more wealthy foreigner would not be noticed amongst the throng.

They found their hotel on the Route des Gaillands, about one kilometre west of the town centre. It was a little alpine hotel in the traditional style; lined throughout with wooden planking and hung with photographs of mountains. Once they had deposited their gear in their room, they headed back downstairs for dinner. Travelling was hungry work and both of them had built up healthy appetites on the drive from Berchtesgaden. Fortunately, the hotel served mountaineer-sized portions of food. Tucking into his tartiflette with all the gusto of a starving gorilla, Danny nevertheless managed to ask the question that had been preying on his mind.

"So…" There was a brief pause for chewing. "What's the plan?"

"Well, the first thing is to take a look at Maric's chalet…" Angus began, before stopping to stare at Danny's sweatshirt. "Before we go any further, can I just compliment you on the artistic distribution of cheese and bacon you have achieved on your top. It goes remarkably well with yesterday's Sauerkraut."

Danny glanced down.

"Thanks very much. It does go well, doesn't it? You were telling me the plan…?"

"Oh, yeah. After dinner, we'll head into town and have a look at this chalet. If we are right and the crates we found at Berchtesgaden contained plundered artworks, then there's a good chance he won't be at home. He'll be off trying to sell his loot to the highest bidder."

"Oh no! Not again!" said Danny, his eyes narrowing in suspicion.

"What?"

"You're planning a burglary, aren't you?"

"I wouldn't call it 'burglary', exactly…"

"No? What would you call it?"

"Just a bit of light breaking and entering. Trust me, he won't even know I've been in."

"Do you remember what happened the last time you did a bit of 'light breaking and entering'? Me, Chief Inspector Newby and a team of crack Senegalese Police officers had to rescue you from an exploding warehouse."

"This is a completely different situation," said Angus, grinning. "This time, I'll have a lookout."

"Yeah, I was afraid you were going to say something like that."

Maric's chalet was north-west of the town centre at the top of a long, steep road lined with expensive-looking houses. It was very old and very big, with walls that had settled into uneven lines and weather-beaten wooden shutters that had kept out countless alpine winters. The mountain rose directly behind it; a thick forest of fir trees and broken crags that stretched upwards into the night. Danny and Angus had found a dark alleyway about fifty yards away and, ducking into its shadows, were eyeing-up the chalet with their spot of light breaking and entering in mind.

"It looks pretty ancient," whispered Danny. "Maybe it won't be that hard to get into?"

"It does look quite old," agreed Angus "but if you look carefully, those windows are all modern double glazing and will no doubt be fitted with high-quality locks which can only be opened from inside. There might even be an alarm. No, it doesn't look like there's any way of getting in through a window without breaking the glass. I'd prefer not do that, as it would tell Maric someone has been poking around and I'd much rather keep him in ignorance. If he suspects someone is onto him, he'll hide the art somewhere we'll never find it. The front door is just as bad; it's right on the road and in the full view of passers-by. No chance of picking the lock without someone noticing. The only good sign is that there are no lights on in the chalet; it seems like there's no-one home."

"So, what are we going to do?" said Danny.

"I'm going to have a look at the back. There might be a rear entrance whose lock I can pick without being seen."

"Do you want me to come too?"

"No, I need you here, to keep a look out. If Maric or one of his thugs arrive, send me a text on your mobile and let me know what's happening."

"No problem."

Angus stepped out of the alleyway into the street and walked casually towards the chalet. With his Raffles Kit thrown nonchalantly over one shoulder, he looked for all the world like someone heading home after a hard day at work. Reaching the alley that ran alongside the chalet, he turned down it without looking to see if he was being watched. If there was one thing that was guaranteed to arouse suspicion, it was looking around furtively like a pantomime villain.

Reaching the rear of the chalet he grimaced with disappointment. There was no back door and, as far as he could see – it was quite dark back there – all the windows were modern double-glazed units, just like those in the front. He considered throwing a boulder through one of the windows, hoping that Maric would think it had simply fallen from one of the crags above, but dismissed the idea: the mountainside wasn't quite steep enough for that to be realistic.

He rubbed the two-day growth of beard on his

chin thoughtfully and inspected the chalet again; there must be some way in. The only other features at the rear of the building were a low woodshed at one side and a drainpipe in the opposite corner, neither of which seemed to offer any advantage to the burglar. Standing on top of the woodshed he'd be able to reach one of the first-floor windows, but it was a double-glazed unit exactly like the ones on the ground floor. Similarly, the drainpipe would allow him to reach windows on all four floors of the chalet, but again, these all appeared to be as modern as the others and he would only be able to open them by smashing the glass.

Suddenly he realised that the drainpipe also offered access to the roof, where there might be a skylight that he could squeeze through. It wouldn't be an easy climb — the eaves of the roof overhung by nearly two metres. Fortunately the drainpipe followed the roof to its edge, in order to reach the guttering.

"Well, no reason to hang about."

Wrapping his hands around the drainpipe, he braced his feet against the wall one after the other and began his climb. It was easy enough to begin with, but as he got higher his arms began to tire and his shoulders ached with the effort. Four storeys is a long way to climb, hand over hand, but at least the drainpipe seemed solid enough.

At last he reached the point where the pipe bent outwards to meet the guttering at the edge of the roof. Angus would have admitted that he was far from comfortable with the next section. Where the drainpipe climbed the wall of the chalet it was secured in place with thick iron bands. Here, it left the wall and reached through space until it connected to the guttering. He had no idea how strong that connection would be and if it broke he would fall a long way to the concrete below. If he got away with broken legs he would be lucky.

With his heart in his mouth he continued along this last section of pipe, his legs swinging free below him. Hand over hand he proceeded slowly towards his destination, willing the pipe to hold his weight. He was a little over half way along when he felt the drainpipe lurch; there was a cracking sound, a groan and the pipe sagged a few centimetres. Flakes of rusty metal fell from the joint between the drainpipe and the gutter, fluttering downwards into the darkness. Angus's heart pounded violently in his chest; he could feel the blood pumping in his ears and the cold shiver of fear scurrying down his spine.

"Hell! Just hold a little while longer!"

If he could just make it these last fifty centimetres, everything would be fine. A few more seconds of effort and suddenly he was there, curling his fingers around solid zinc guttering. He paused for a moment, hanging by his fingers, and breathed a sigh of relief. He wasn't on the roof quite yet, but the worst was definitely over.

Gathering his strength, he swung his right foot up and hooked his heel into the gutter. Then he pulled hard, swinging his bodyweight up and onto the roof. He hung for a moment on the point of balance, pushing down with all his strength on his fingers. At last he managed to hook the toes of his left foot over the edge of the guttering as well and he was up; he had made it onto the roof.

He crouched there for a moment, getting his breath back and feeling the burning pain subside from his arms and shoulders. He became aware of the cold wind biting into his sweat-soaked clothes and the greasiness of the tiles under his fingers. He would have to be careful how he moved around.

Examining his elevated surroundings, he noted with disappointment that there were no skylights on this side of the roof. At the apex, however, was a chimney stack, which he decided to climb up to. He doubted it would provide a way in, but from there he would be able to see if there were any skylights on the other side. Gingerly, he made his way up the slippery tiles until he reached the chimneys, where he sat down, a leg on either side of the roof.

Below him were stretched the glimmering lights of Chamonix and above were the dark, stiletto silhouettes of mountains. In between, in the dark recesses below the peaks, shone the occasional lonely lights of mountain refuges. Inside, climbers from all over the world would be sitting around plates of steaming stew, with glasses of rough table-wine in their hands, discussing future plans and past glories. It was, Angus reflected, a far more sensible way of getting your thrills than climbing the treacherous drainpipes of Neo-Nazi thugs.

Looking down, Angus could see that there were no skylights on the other side of the roof either. Inspecting the chimney stack, he confirmed that it would not provide a way into the chalet; the chimneys were all quite narrow and he was no Santa Claus. It appeared he had climbed the drainpipe for nothing.

Carefully, he began his descent back to where the drainpipe met the guttering. It was a nerve-wracking experience; there were no hand or foot holds and the slates were covered in a slippery combination of wet moss and green algae.

He was about halfway to the guttering when his foot dislodged a loose slate. It slid out from under him as soon as he put his weight on it, skittering down the roof and shooting over the edge. A moment's silence was followed by loud crack, as it shattered on the ground below. Angus very nearly lost his balance, but somehow managed to hold on. For the second time that night, his heart beat wildly and he felt his scalp tighten with fear.

He quickly calmed himself, however, and was soon inspecting with curiosity the gap where the slate had been. Under the slates, as with most roofs, was a layer of planks. These would be attached to the rafters that provided the framework of the roof. Each slate was attached to the planking with a single nail through the top. Angus could see that the planks were old and rough; over the years they had contracted and warped leaving noticeable gaps between them. A thought occurred to him and he smiled slowly in the darkness. Perhaps there was a way into this chalet after all.

Shrugging off the Raffles Kit, he rummaged about

inside it and, after a few moments, produced a large screwdriver. With this he started to prise off the slates one by one. The nails which held the tiles were very old and rusty, but could be pulled out with a little patience. He was careful not to break them as he would need them to reattach the tiles after he had finished his 'light breaking and entering'.

Once he had cleared the tiles from an area of about sixty centimetres squared, he then went to work on the planking. Sliding a hacksaw blade from his kit into a gap between two planks, he began to saw. It was hard work; the hacksaw blade had small teeth and was made for cutting metal, which meant it made very slow progress through the wood. After about half an hour, however, he had cut out three sections of plank, making a hole just big enough for him to squeeze through.

Pulling his little key-ring torch from his pocket, he shone the beam into the entrance he had made for himself. The narrow shaft of white light swept across ancient wooden joists with modern fibreglass insulation in between; this was clearly the chalet's attic space. It did not appear to be used for anything and was thick with dust and cobwebs.

Angus lowered himself carefully through

the hole, being careful to place his feet on the joists below him. The insulation probably lay directly on a plaster ceiling which would not bear his weight. If anything was sure to alert Maric to the fact someone had been poking around his house, it was a burglar-shaped hole in the ceiling.

Once inside, he stepped carefully from joist to joist, searching for the hatch that would lead down into the house. He found it at the far end of the attic; a small wooden square so deep in dust he thought it must have been many years since it was last used.

Switching off his torch, Angus pulled the hatch open and then stopped to listen. He gave it a full minute before he switched it back on: he wanted to be quite sure that there was no-one at home. When he was satisfied, he pointed the torch down into the chalet. Below was a long, narrow corridor. The only furnishings were a sideboard, sitting against the wall under the hatch (handy, thought Angus, for climbing back up on his way out) and heavy oriental carpets spread loosely over the dark, highly-polished floorboards. There were several doors off the corridor and at the far end, a staircase leading down. Angus lowered himself through the hatch until he was hanging by his fingertips, then dropped lightly to floor below.

It was a huge house and he realised he would have to search efficiently if he was to find anything which implicated Maric in the dealing of illegal art or that connected him to the Adler Kommando. The first thing to look for was some kind of office or study, as that would be the most likely place to find incriminating evidence.

He moved fast, on his tip-toes, his trainers making no sound on the thick carpets. Opening each door in turn, he shone the torch directly at the floor. This way there was enough reflected light to see what was in the room, but he was not flashing the beam around the walls and alerting anyone passing by outside that a burglar was at work.

Making his way through the chalet, he dismissed room after room as being of no interest; they were all bedrooms, bathrooms or drawing rooms. A couple of rooms were piled up with furniture and boxes of junk, and required closer inspection, but it seemed they were just store rooms for un-used items. On the first floor, however, he came to a library.

Apart from where another door led out of the room to his left, the room was completely lined with shelves of books as high as the ceiling. Some of the books were old, with dark leather bindings and titles picked out in gold; others were obviously much newer and had glossy, multi-coloured spines. All of them appeared to be text-books, histories or biographies; he could see no fiction at all. On a whim, Angus ran his eyes over the shelves till he found the letter H. On the third shelf up he found what he was looking for.

"Mein Kampf. Hmph!" he muttered under his breath, "No surprise there." Taking a couple of paces to his right he found the 'L's: "Martin Luther… aye, you can tell a lot about a man from his bookshelves!" Another step and there, on a high shelf, was confirmation of his suspicions: "Nietzsche! Well if this guy's not a Nazi, then he's got the full set of instruction manuals!"

He turned to the table which sat in the centre of the room. It was a peculiar-looking thing: a large, square chunk of Victorian grandeur that looked like it would have taken half a dozen strong men with handlebar moustaches to move. The top was heavily scarred with dents and pin-pricks and on either side were wide, shallow drawers with brass handles.

In fact, Angus knew exactly what it was. He had seen something very similar in the Royal Geographic

Society in London: it was a map-table. The pin-pricks in the top would have been made by navigational dividers and the wide, shallow drawers were so you could store your maps without folding or rolling them. It occurred to Angus that these drawers might make a good place to hide some stolen paintings.

He started with the top drawer on the left hand side of the table, pulling it open with a jerk. Inside, disappointingly — but not surprisingly — were maps. Covering Western Europe, they dated from the 1930s and looked military. The drawer below contained maritime charts of the Baltic Sea. In the third drawer, however, he struck gold. In a medium-sized leather portfolio, separated by sheets of tissue paper, was a collection of around twenty works of art. They were mostly sketches; life drawings of muscular men in dramatic poses: shielding their eyes, begging forgiveness or dying from some unknown malady. The rest were watercolours: a couple of thunderously dramatic seascapes and an alpine meadow, bathed in golden sunshine.

Angus would never claim to be an expert in the arts, but he thought the pictures looked to be of the highest quality. The confidence of the lines, the perfection of the bodily proportions, the way the light fell on the waves and in the meadow — these were valuable all right. How valuable he didn't know, but he would guess they were worth several thousand pounds each. Together they would be worth a great deal, perhaps over a hundred thousand pounds.

A quick check through the remaining drawers revealed nothing else of interest. Angus was puzzled. There had been several quite large crates in the cave at Berchtesgaden but none of these pictures were big enough to warrant crates of that size, even if they had originally been in frames. Of course, there was a chance that the pictures that had been in the crates were just too large to fit in the map-table and had been stored somewhere else.

Looking around, Angus decided that there was nowhere that would provide a suitable hiding place for one large painting, never mind several. They must be somewhere else in the house. He strode over to the library's other door and flung it open impatiently. With every extra minute he spent in the house, his chances of being discovered increased.

What he found took him completely by surprise. Firstly because, despite the imposing doorway, it wasn't another room, it was just a cupboard. Secondly, because right in front of him was what he had been hoping to find: six full-sized oil paintings still in their original frames. A brief chuckle escaped from his lips as he inspected them more closely; here was some serious artwork.

The first two were landscapes: rich, rolling farmland sprinkled with trees and cattle. The rest were portraits. Three were fairly skilful depictions of chubby renaissance ladies disporting themselves in the altogether, but the last was in a different league. It was of a young man, gazing directly at the artist, the merest suggestion of self-consciousness in the startling clarity of his eyes. It took Angus's breath away. He had no idea what it's monetary worth might be, but in terms of sheer artistic beauty, it was priceless. For a few seconds he gazed transfixed.

Then, breaking the spell, his mobile phone (which he had switched to silent mode for obvious reasons) began to vibrate urgently in his pocket. Remembering suddenly where he was, he snatched the phone out of his jacket and opened the message that Danny had sent him. This could be a warning of imminent danger.

Big cow herd. It is Maria.

It had to be said, it wasn't what he'd been expecting. Puzzled, he thumbed in his reply.

What in hell u talking about?

While he waited for an answer he took the opportunity to photograph the paintings with his mobile phone. When he got a moment, he would email the pictures to his old friend Chief Inspector Newby at New Scotland Yard. Newby might be able to discover where they came from and if they really had been looted by the Nazis during the war.

If so, the value of the paintings would be reduced by the fact that they could not be sold on the open market, but Angus imagined that they could still be worth a fortune – over a million pounds perhaps? He felt his phone vibrate again.

Sorry, Big bmw here. Maric.

"Damn predictive text," Angus muttered, realising Danny's mistake.

At that moment a key rattled in a lock and voices could be heard. He ran quickly but silently out of the library, making for the staircase. Reaching it, he peered over the banister to the ground floor.

Below him, removing their coats and scarves and hanging them on hooks in the hallway, were three men. One was Nikola Maric, the other two he had never seen before. They looked different to Maric: more sharply dressed. Gold watches flashed at their wrists and under their long woollen coats they wore beautifully tailored Italian suits. Suits, Angus noted, that had been cut to hang a little looser around the left armpit.

One was short and fat and red in face; in the way of a man who eats and drinks too much, without getting any exercise to burn it off. The other was taller with a fitter build; he had a pinched, rat-like face, with a nose that had been broken into a twisted hook. His hands looked too large for the rest of him and hung like heavy weights by his sides. They were an ugly pair of goons, and their cashmere coats, designer suits and gold watches just made them seem all the uglier.

Angus had investigated the sophisticated thuggery of organised crime before and could smell dirty money a mile off. It was a weakness he had observed in many gangsters; the need to display their wealth with the purchase of expensive clothes, fancy consumer goods and luxury cars. They were just the kind of guys to be interested in buying some illegal art.

Having hung up their coats, the three men started up the stairs. Angus realised he had a real problem. He could not get back to the attic in order to make his escape as that would require climbing the stairs; and as soon as he tried that, he would be spotted by Maric and the gangsters lower down.

He had just a few seconds, there was no time to think: he had to act now. Quickly and quietly he retraced his steps to the library and ducked inside, closing the door behind him. Seconds later he heard footsteps in the hall outside, heading in his direction.

He cursed himself for a fool; if these men were here to buy the art from Maric, he would obviously take them to where it was hidden! His stupidity had trapped him; if only he had chosen one of the other rooms on the landing!

He did all he could in the circumstances; darting to the cupboard which held the larger oil paintings, he ducked inside and shut the door behind him. He was only just in time; as he pulled the door closed he heard the handle of the library door being turned. Standing in the perfect darkness, trying to breathe as quietly as possible, he heard voices. They were talking English, which must have been their common language.

"...of course I can show you. I do not expect you to take me at my word!" It was Maric's voice, Angus recognised it from the night he had met him in Dunkeld.

"Excellent, Mister Maric!" Came the reply in a rich, deep voice; the speaker rolling his 'r's musically. The accent was unmistakeably Russian. "I am excited to see these paintings. If they are what you say they are, it is truly a wonderful opportunity."

"Oh, they are the real thing my friend! Vodka?"

"That would be good. Vasily?"

A third voice, also Russian, said, "Yes, boss."

Angus guessed that the short, fat gangster was the boss and the taller one was his bodyguard. It seemed that his suspicion that they were here to view the artwork was confirmed. In which case, it was only a matter of time before Maric opened the cupboard to show them the oil paintings, discovering Angus in the process. He was just considering which of the contents of his Raffles Kit would make the most effective weapon, when he was struck with an idea. Pulling out his mobile he thumbed in a message for Danny.

Am trapped. Create disturbance to draw Maric out of house.

He smiled in the darkness. If Danny could attract Maric's attention and get him out of the house, Angus could take the opportunity to slip out the way he'd come in. He couldn't think of a way Danny could do this off the top of his head, but he was sure the lad would come up with something.

Glasses clinked in the library.

"Na zdorovje!"

"Na zdorovje!" the others repeated.

There was a brief pause, then Maric spoke again.

"Come. I will show you the sketches first. They are extremely fine, I think you will agree."

Angus heard a drawer being slid open and the metallic buzz of a zip; then another pause. After a few minutes, the Russian gangster's voice broke the silence.

"These are very fine indeed! It seems you are true to your word! Now… what about the paintings? They are what I am really here to see!"

"Of course, in just a moment. First, I would like to confirm that we have a deal. The agent will be in Krakow as agreed?"

Angus froze. He stopped breathing. Even his heart seemed to stop pumping as his whole being strained to hear what was being said. He had assumed the paintings would simply be sold for cash. He had not considered that they would be exchanged for something else. Who on earth was 'the agent'?

Were the paintings some kind of ransom? Perhaps Maric had been spying on the Russians and his agent had been caught? No, that was ridiculous; the Russians would simply have killed anyone found spying on their interests. And their manner was far too cordial for that; they seemed more like friendly businessmen striking a deal.

It was more likely that Maric was buying some service, which the agent could supply. But what kind of service could possibly be worth handing over so much valuable art for? Angus doubted it was for the greater good.

"If the paintings, like the sketches, are as you described; then we have a deal. We will bring the agent to Krakow on the 21st of April and make the exchange at the bend of the river, right below the castle walls — as we agreed," replied the Russian.

"Excellent! Then let me show you the paintings. I guarantee you will not be disappointed!"

Angus readied himself as he realised Maric was just a few seconds from opening the door and discovering him. What on earth was the boy playing at? Surely it couldn't be that difficult to arrange some kind of distraction.

Footsteps echoed on the library floor, getting louder

as they approached. Angus thought about the bulges under the Russian's left armpits and wondered what kind of handguns they were packing. Enormous silver cannons with pearl handles, if his experience of gangsters was anything to go by.

He pulled the big screwdriver from his Raffles Kit — not much of a weapon to face enormous silver cannons with but it was all he had. The footsteps stopped. Angus took a deep breath and made ready to lunge.

CHAPTER SIX

Only a few minutes ago, before Maric had arrived with the two men who looked like gangsters, Danny had been cursing the job of lookout as the most boring in the world. Now, it was all getting a little too interesting.

He had thought about texting Angus back and asking him what exactly he'd meant by 'a disturbance', but had decided it was only likely to result in a terse reply, probably one consisting largely of four letter words. No, this was a time for independent action.

He stared up the street towards the chalet. What would draw Maric and his friends outside? What would get *him* to go outside on a cold night like this? Knocking on the door and shouting "Ooh, look at the fireworks! Aren't they pretty?" He frowned at his own stupidity. That was hardly likely to bring hardened criminals like Maric and his cronies bursting from the front door wearing wide-eyed looks of boyish wonder.

If Maric had been alone it would have been simple – he could have rung the doorbell and run off.

But Maric was not alone and he needed to think of something that would draw all three of them out of the house- something that would really catch their attention.

His eyes fell upon the expensive BMW which was now parked outside the chalet and suddenly he had an idea. A car like that was sure to have an alarm...

He left the cover of the alley and ran to where the car was parked. Climbing on to the rear bumper, he jumped up and down, rocking it violently on its suspension.

Nothing. Not the slightest parp or whistle from the bouncing vehicle. If the car had an alarm, it wasn't very sensitive. Perhaps he would have to be a bit more aggressive to set it off.

Looking around for a loose rock, he found one that had fallen from a nearby wall; it was about the size of an orange and perfect for his purposes. Raising the rock in his right hand, he flung it as hard as he could at the window next to the driver's seat. The window exploded in a shower of tiny crystal fragments and a loud 'Bang!' echoed down the empty street. Danny turned, making ready to sprint away, but hesitated. Silence reigned again: it seemed the car wasn't fitted with an alarm after all. He waited to see if the noise of the breaking window had been heard inside the chalet, but no faces came to the window, no indignant shouts rang through the night.

"Damn it!" he said loudly — there didn't seem much point in staying quiet any more. This was a real problem. Angus was in the house the gangsters had entered and the fact that he had texted meant the situation was critical. Angus didn't do practical jokes in this sort of situation. If he'd asked for a 'disturbance' then his need was urgent. His life might depend on it.

Danny stared sullenly at the BMW. What kind of person would buy a car as expensive as this one and not fit an alarm? It was stupid. In fact it wasn't just stupid, it was downright inconsiderate. Well, whether Maric liked it or not, he was going to create a disturbance with this car if he had to set the flippin' thing on fire! He looked again at the car and grinned; suddenly it had all become very clear.

Rushing forward, he stuck his head and shoulders through the broken window, searching the controls in the dim orange light thrown by a nearby streetlamp. In a few seconds he had found what he was hunting for: the lever that opened the petrol-cap cover. He gave it a tug and heard a click as it popped open.

Now he just needed to find the bonnet release. After a few long and frustrating seconds he found it; tucked away in the darkness under the steering wheel. The bonnet opened with a dull clunk.

Danny felt suddenly light-headed as a confusing mixture of emotions battled for supremacy. On the one hand he felt a terrible fear for Angus's safety and a rising panic that he wasn't working fast enough. On the other, he felt a surge of excitement that was almost overwhelming. He wondered, briefly, if it was okay to be rather enjoying a situation in which his uncle was in deadly peril. Taking a deep breath, he calmed himself down and got back to the job in hand.

Dashing to the rear of the car, he hurriedly unscrewed the petrol cap. Taking off his scarf, he pushed one end down into the petrol tank and kept pushing until only a short length remained dangling down the side of the car. Next, he lifted up the bonnet. The next bit was tricky, he had to make a spark using the car battery, but wasn't quite sure how to do it. What he needed was a length of wire. There were plenty of wires under the bonnet, but they were all securely attached to bits of engine and he had no tools to disconnect them.

He stood motionless, staring at nothing as he thought hard. There must be something he could use... his iPod! He pulled the music player from his pocket and disconnected the headphones. Gripping one of the earpieces in his teeth, he pulled hard on the wire.

"Ow!" He spat the earpiece out onto the road. Biting it off had hurt his teeth, but it had served its purpose: where the earpiece had been was now an exposed end of copper wire. His hands shook with excitement and anxiety. In his hurry, he dropped the wire on the ground.

"Keep calm, keep calm!" he said to himself, picking it up. His plan was nearly complete and he hadn't heard any gun-shots or screams yet, so maybe he still had enough time. Pulling the plastic covers from the car's battery terminals, he wrapped the exposed end of the wire round the positive terminal.

"Now... let's see if this works!"

Slowly, he brought the jack-plug of the 'phones closer to the negative terminal of the car battery. When it was a few millimetres from the terminal, tiny blue sparks crackled between them and a little puff of white smoke rose into the air. It wasn't quite what he'd been hoping for: he'd expected the sparks to be much stronger. However, a spark was a spark and ought to do the job he required of it — the plan might just work!

Pulling his scarf from the petrol tank, he noted with satisfaction that it had soaked up a good deal of petrol. Carrying it forward to the front of the car, he placed it carefully over the negative terminal of the battery.

He took a deep breath. This was it: the moment of truth. Picking up the wire again, he brought the jack-plug towards the corner of scarf which lay over the terminal. He held it closer, then a little closer still, then a little closer …

"WHOOMF!"

A sudden explosion flashed under the bonnet of the car. Danny reeled backwards as the heat of the blast washed over his face. The acrid smell of his own burnt hair filled his nostrils and he covered his face with his arms. Backing away a couple of paces, he risked a look at the car.

He had succeeded beyond his wildest hopes. The scarf was blazing away fiercely, thick clouds of smoke belching up into the night sky. Running forward, he grabbed the end which had not been soaked with petrol and was not yet burning. Pulling the scarf out from under the bonnet, he hurled it in through the broken car window.

It did not take long for the flames to catch. In less than a minute the car's upholstery was blazing, throwing up a heavy pall of poisonous black smoke. Soon the flames were licking out of the window, blistering the paint and threatening to engulf the car completely.

Running to the door of the chalet, Danny searched his memory for the right French words – he thought speaking English might warn Maric that he and Angus were on his trail. Unfortunately, the small amount of French he'd learnt at school wasn't really intended for this sort of situation. Hammering loudly on the heavy door, he decided he'd just have to do his best and hope they didn't notice.

"Monsieur! Attention! Votre voiture! C'est une… flambé!"

Then he ran off down the street, heading for the safety of the alley. He only just made it in time; as he ducked into its protective shadows he heard the door of the chalet bang open and a terrible roar of anger. Risking a peek round the corner, he saw Maric and the two goons silhouetted by the growing inferno. All three of them had handguns drawn and were looking around wildly for someone to shoot. They were shouting at each other but, despite the fact they seemed to be yelling in English, he struggled to hear what was being said. The few words he did hear, he would not have repeated in polite company.

He decided it was time to leave. The three men had split up and were spreading out; presumably to hunt for a culprit. Walking straight towards him was the shorter of the two gangsters. He was a chubby little man whom Danny would not normally have found very frightening. However, the enormous silver handgun in his right hand looked like it was designed to bring down helicopters. Danny pulled out his mobile and sent a quick final message to Angus:

Have created disturbance, c u at hotel.

Then, turning on his heel, he walked hurriedly down the alley, away from the approaching gangster. About twenty metres down he turned a corner and relaxed a little. Stopping in a doorway, he listened for sounds that might indicate the gangster was searching the alley. For a few seconds he stood, motionless, listening to the night. All he could hear was the muted murmur of a television in one of the nearby houses.

He was just about to continue on his way when he heard the slap of shoe-leather on concrete and a whispered curse; exactly as though someone had tripped in the darkness. He held his breath and listened again… waiting for confirmation of his fears. Then he heard it: the soft shuffle of approaching footsteps.

This was no time to hang around; stepping out of the doorway he hurried off down the alley, trying to reach a compromise between speed and silence. He had gone about fifty metres when the shout came.

"HEY!"

He threw a quick look backwards. At the corner of the alley stood a dark figure, gun raised and pointing straight at him. Time to run. He broke into a sprint, ducking and twisting to throw off the gangster's aim.

"BOOM!" The noise of the gun echoed from the walls of the alley; absurdly loud in the enclosed space. A bullet ripped into the wall next to him; tearing away a huge chunk of mortar and showering him with debris.

Danny cursed and ducked for cover. Getting shot at was definitely one of his least favourite things in life. He sprinted on, running as fast as he ever had.

"BOOM!" Another bullet whistled down the alley

and struck something ahead of him with a metallic bang. Danny could see the end of the alley now. It came to a junction with another road about one hundred long metres ahead. There was no way he could reach the end without getting shot; he was like the proverbial fish in a barrel. His only hope lay in the doors that faced onto the alley: perhaps someone would have left one open.

He slammed his shoulder into the first door, twisting at its handle with desperate fingers. It did not open.

"BOOM!" Another bullet smashed into the brickwork by his head; the gangster was getting closer with every shot. The next one might find its mark.

There was another door almost opposite. Lunging across the alley he reached frantically for the handle and twisted: it burst open and he fell inside. He was on his feet in an instant, wondering which way to go – down the hall or up the stairs? At that moment a frail-looking old woman appeared at the top of the stairs, brandishing her walking stick like a weapon.

"Qu'est ce que vous voulez?" She was trying to sound firm, but her voice trembled; she was clearly terrified. Danny stared at her, trying to remember the correct French words. He blurted out a sentence hoping it would make some kind of sense.

"Bonsoir, madame. Vous avez une porte dans le… um… derriere?"

"Pourquoi?"

"Pardonez-moi. Les Nazis…Bang! Bang!" This conversation was getting damn silly. At last he found the right words. "Madame. Avez vous une autre sortie?"

"Les Nazis?" She looked horrified and confused. "Mais oui! Vite…" She pointed Danny to a door that exited the hall on his left. He dived through it, hoping he hadn't given the old dear a heart attack. He found himself in a sitting room, then a tiny kitchen, on the other side of which was a door. Crashing through it, he emerged into another alley. He took to his heels, flying over the uneven concrete like it was a running track.

Glancing behind him, he saw the gangster come running out of the door. The man stopped and leaned against a wall, apparently exhausted by the pursuit. It was the last Danny saw of him. The next second he turned a corner and found himself on a busy street which led into the centre of town. Slowing to a fast walk he ducked into a group of tourists, hiding in the anonymity of the crowd. Even if the gangster was to follow him into the street, Danny doubted he'd seen enough of him to be able pick him out of a group. To be on the safe side, he removed his jacket and slung it over his shoulder. Thus disguised, he made his way back to the hotel, stopping occasionally to check behind for gun-wielding thugs.

Once back in the hotel-room, Danny collapsed onto his bed and waited for Angus to return. It was an anxious wait, but thankfully not a long one. After just a few minutes Angus burst enthusiastically into their room. He was grinning from ear to ear.

"Hell! That was too close for comfort!" he said.

"You're not kidding," replied Danny.

"Nice work on the disturbance front; your timing was perfect! Maric was just about to find my hiding place when you banged on his door."

"Don't mention it. You owe me a set of headphones, a scarf and very probably a new pair of underpants."

"No problem. I must say, I wasn't expecting anything quite so spectacular…" Angus paused, peering closely at Danny's face. "Where are your eyebrows?"

"I sacrificed them in the name of investigative journalism. I had no idea petrol was so explosive."

Angus laughed. "Well, now you know! Another wee lesson to add to your life experience! By the way, did I hear gunshots while I was escaping from the chalet?"

"Yes, you did. I got chased by one of the gangsters. He was carrying a pocket flipping Howitzer. I am sodding lucky to be alive! If Social Services knew just half of the stuff you put me through..."

"Sorry about that. Lookout is usually a pretty safe job."

"Never mind. It's better than being at..." Danny stopped himself just in time. Angus seemed to have forgotten that Danny should have been back at school several days ago. "Um... so what did you find out? Any pictures?"

Angus told Danny how he had eventually found a way into the chalet and discovered the art in the library. He went on to relate how he had been trapped in the cupboard with the paintings and had overheard Maric and the Russians strike a deal.

"Maric was just about to open the cupboard when you hammered on his front door. If you'd been two seconds later, he would have found me. When he ran out, followed by the Russians, I left by the way I came in.

"I've put the roof back together with the help of some duct tape, but I don't expect it will survive more than a couple of heavy downpours. Hopefully, he won't notice the hole until this whole thing's over. That way he won't know we're onto him."

"What about the car? Won't torching the car make him a little suspicious?" asked Danny.

"Maybe. But, with any luck, he'll just think it was some out-of-control kids on an alco-pop fuelled rampage. The fact that one of the Russians saw a shifty youth running off down the street should encourage that belief."

"'Shifty'? Thanks very much!" said Danny. "So what next?"

Angus smiled and rubbed his hands together happily.

CHAPTER SEVEN

Danny stood in Krakow's main square, gazing up at the Wieza Ratuszowa tower.

"Nice city, isn't it?" he said, glancing over at Angus, who was looking up at the same building with admiration.

"Aye, a bit like Prague in some ways. Very unspoilt… hardly a modern building to be seen."

It was true, Krakow looked like it could not have changed a great deal in the last few hundred years. There seemed to be ancient churches, colleges and markets everywhere they looked. The astronomer Copernicus, if he could somehow have been miraculously brought back to life, would probably still have recognized the streets he had walked in the fifteenth century when he had declared that the sun was stationary at the centre of the solar system.

They wandered down one of the narrow streets which led off from the central square, in the hunt for something to eat. They still had a couple of hours before Maric was due to meet with the Russians and Angus had suggested they use the time constructively.

Walking along stone-flagged streets, under tall, regal looking buildings with elegantly decorated facades, they paused at last by the dimly-lit entrance to a narrow covered alleyway. There was a sign bearing the word Restauracja and an arrow pointing down the alley.

"This might offer a little local colour!" said Angus, setting off in the direction of the arrow. After about thirty metres, a narrow flight of steps curled down into the earth, ending at a heavy wooden door. Angus tugged on the iron handle and it groaned slowly open with an eerie haunted-house creak.

Inside, it was much cosier than the dingy alley hinted it might be. A bar sat against one wall and along the others were small, wooden booths. The walls were bare brick and arched to a point high above their heads. A collection of old paintings and a thick red carpet gave it a surprisingly homely feel.

They ordered goulash, which came in bowls made from loaves of chewy bread. The meat was beautifully tender, the sauce was spiced to perfection and it came in portions that more than assuaged their hunger. Taking a long suck on his cola, Danny wiped his mouth with his sleeve and broke the silence that often descends when hungry men are presented with bread and meat.

"I'm assuming you have a plan beyond eating and drinking?"

"You should know me better than that by now," said Angus with a grin. "Seriously though, I don't think we have enough information to make a proper plan. We know where and when they are going to meet, but that's about it. We'll head down to the river shortly and check the area out. I've brought my binoculars in case we can't get close. We don't want to advertise our presence to Maric, of course, so I think it would be a good idea to wear hats or something that we can pull low over our faces."

"I've got my beanie with me," said Danny.

"Hmm. It's a bit warm for woolly hats. Wearing one would probably draw attention to yourself. We'll nip into a sports shop on the way down and get a couple of baseball caps."

Angus stood up and drained the final dregs of his cola.

"Jings, that was a good feed. I think I'm going to like Poland." He glanced at his watch. "We should get going; we want to be down there in plenty of time."

★ ★ ★

The quiet path that ran along the banks of the River Vistula and below the high walls of Krakow Castle — the 'Wawel' as the locals called it — seemed like the most likely spot for Maric and the Russians to perform the exchange. It was a secluded spot and ideal for dodgy dealings between gangsters. Danny wondered what the agent would look like. He'd never seen a spy before, unless you counted Newby, and he hadn't been a spy for a very long time.

Maybe he'd be a slick James Bond type wearing a Savile Row suit, Italian shoes and a watch that contained a miniature nuclear bomb, a garrotte and a device for getting beautiful women out of cocktail dresses. He would just have to wait and see.

They walked slowly, like tourists enjoying the view. Every now and then they would turn and gaze up at the castle, perhaps pointing at one of the towers to embellish their masquerade as sightseers. It was dark now, of course, but the castle was well-lit, so it was perfectly reasonable for tourists to be walking on the riverbank.

At ten to nine there was still no sign of Maric or the Russians. In fact, Danny and Angus seemed to be the only people about. The only others nearby were dining in a riverboat restaurant moored by the path, a little upstream of the castle. About fifty yards from the bend in the river below the castle they found a bench which offered a good view of the path. They sat down and waited for something to happen.

The Wawel loomed above them, lending an air of drama to the proceedings, its high walls and steeply pitched roofs climbing precipitously into the night sky. It looked powerful and invulnerable, thought Danny, yet elegant in a way that British castles rarely were. If the castles of home evoked images of grubby soldiers pouring boiling oil over battlements and blowing each other up with cannons, the delicate spires of the Wawel made him think of men in powdered wigs embroiling themselves in Machiavellian politics: blackmail, betrayal and murder by poison…

His thoughts were interrupted by Angus, who had grabbed his arm suddenly and pointed in the direction of the Vistula. There, cruising slowly on the black water, was a small cabin-cruiser. At its wheel stood a dark figure whose white face stared resolutely forward, oblivious to the spectacular castle above them. Angus lifted his binoculars to get a better look.

"Maric!" he hissed. "It never occurred to me the exchange would take place on the river!"

The noise of the boat's engine dropped to a muted throbbing, then cut out altogether. The boat still had plenty of momentum, however, and glided on — cutting a smooth v-shaped wake through the dark, glass-like surface of the river. It was heading downstream, towards a concrete road-bridge that crossed the river four hundred metres away.

"Where is he going?" asked Danny. "Aren't they meant to be meeting at the bend of the river?"

"I don't know… wait a minute! Look!" He pointed past the cabin cruiser to a dark shape that sat by the opposite bank. It was a river-barge, moored a discreet distance from any buildings and about thirty metres from the concrete road bridge. As they watched, Maric steered his boat towards the barge and slowly brought it to a halt alongside. A figure appeared on the deck of the barge and threw Maric a rope. A few seconds later, two men appeared from the cabin of Maric's boat and the three of them then clambered onto the barge before disappearing down into its dark hulk. Angus grimaced.

"We've got to get closer!" he said. "We need to be able to see and hear what's going on. Come on!"

They walked briskly down to the riverbank and along the path in the direction of the barge. A couple of minutes saw them standing on the path opposite where the barge was moored. They stared across at it in frustration: the river was about a hundred metres wide here and the barge was moored to the opposite bank. They could still see very little and could, of course, hear nothing. While they were wondering what to do next there was the bang of a door being opened and a flurry of movement on the barge. They caught the sound of instructions being given and of heavy objects being moved.

"Quick, we can't stand here gawping," said Angus, grabbing Danny by the elbow and leading him.

They were not a moment too soon; just as they disappeared into the shadow of a tree's branches, Maric appeared on deck and looked around suspiciously. Seeing nothing of concern, he grunted something to the men below and jumped down into the cabin cruiser.

Moments later his cronies formed a line and passed objects from man to man, from the barge to the cabin-cruiser. Angus peered once more through his binoculars. The shape of the objects was unmistakable.

"Strange. They seem to be loading canisters of some sort onto the cabin-cruiser," he told Danny, "Gas canisters, by the look of them."

"Gas canisters?" replied Danny. "What are they for?"

"I have no idea," admitted Angus.

Within a few minutes they had finished loading the canisters and Maric's men now passed a portfolio case and two large wooden crates from the cabin-cruiser to the barge. Once this was done, they all clambered onto the barge and disappeared down into its cabin.

"The paintings!" whispered Danny hoarsely; this whole thing was proving to be very mysterious. He wondered what would happen next, but would have freely admitted that he could never have guessed Angus's next move.

"I'm going for a swim," said Angus.

"Eh?" said Danny.

"I might never get a better chance to find out what's in those canisters. If I swim the river under the bridge I'll be in pitch black shadow; no-one will be able to see me. Come on, I'll need you to take care of my clothes. We'd better hurry, they could finish their business at any moment."

They ran the short distance to the bridge and

ducked into the shadow below. Quickly stripping down to his boxer-shorts, Angus made ready to slip into the water.

"Right, Danny, you stay here and look after my stuff. Keep an eye on the barge, if anything untoward happens… well, deal with it as you see fit."

"No problem."

"Try not to get kidnapped or anything, okay?"

"I'll do my best."

"Good."

"Oh, Angus?"

"Yes, what is it?"

"Nice boxers… are those little love-hearts?"

"They were a present."

"Really? Who from?"

"I think it would be best if you maintained absolute silence from now on."

With that, Angus slipped quietly into the water and swam in a slow, but silent, breast-stroke towards the opposite bank. Reaching the other side, he stopped and trod water for a moment. The shadow of the bridge only covered a narrow band of river; between him and the barge was twenty-five metres of open water, well lit from nearby streetlamps and the headlights of passing cars. In order not to attract the attention of anyone who happened to come up onto the deck of the barge, he would have to swim this section underwater.

Twenty-five metres is a long way to swim underwater. In a dark and freezing river, it is a difficult task by anyone's standards. Angus took several long, deep breaths, gulping the air into his lungs and saturating his blood with oxygen. It was a trick he'd seen done by pearl-divers in the Polynesian islands and it seemed to work for them.

Taking one final gulp of air, he ducked under and started the long swim to the barge. He swept his arms backwards in long, steady strokes; pulling himself slowly forward through the frigid gloom. Slow and steady – that was the way. Thrashing along impatiently would just mean running out of air too quickly and having to surface before he reached his destination. Even so, it was not long before his chest started to ache; a dull burning sensation that increased with the seconds.

By the time he was half-way there it had spread and intensified and he had developed a sharp pain in the back of his head. With five metres to go he was desperate to take a breath, the pain had spread forward into his eyes and what little vision he had under the water was blurring. *Just a few more strokes!* he thought, pulling himself slowly through the final metres of water. At last his fingers touched something hard and rough; in the darkness he could just make out the curving iron hull of the barge. He allowed himself to float upwards, breaking the surface gratefully with a soft splash.

He sucked the sweet night air down into his lungs with relief and looked around quickly, to see if he had been spotted. However, coming up hard against the hull of the barge, he had surfaced under its bows, in a little pocket of covering shadow. Nobody appeared to have noticed his approach.

He trod water again, for a full minute, getting his breath back after his exertions, then began to work his way slowly along the length of the barge. He discovered that the gunwales of the barge overhung slightly and that, if he stayed close to the hull, he could remain out of sight of anyone who might innocently wander past and wonder why he was swimming around in the darkness dressed in novelty Valentine's Day underwear.

Reaching the point where Maric's boat was tied to the barge, he made his way round to the cabin-cruiser's rear, where its sides were low and close to the water. Pulling himself up, he slipped stealthily over the gunwale and into the boat. In front of him was a small hatchway and, to its right, the steering wheel and some other controls. He crept forward and eased open the hatchway door, peering into the gloomy interior. It was very dark inside and he realised with annoyance that he'd left his little key-ring torch in the pocket of his jeans. He would just have to do his best with the street-lighting which was filtering in through the cabin's portholes.

Fortunately, what he was looking for was right in front of him, stacked neatly into robust steel crates. Grasping one of the canisters by the valve at its top, he eased it from the crate and examined it more closely in the dim amber light. It was military green and covered in black, stencilled writing. Unfortunately the writing was Cyrillic and it was several years since Angus had last spoken any Russian. In fact, the only thing he could remember how to say in the language was 'Please do not kill me.' It was a phrase that might yet prove useful.

He could, however, translate the warning symbol printed next to the writing. It was a triangle containing a skull and crossbones — the international warning symbol for a deadly substance – painted in red, white and black. Whatever was in these canisters was nasty stuff. Angus looked again at the writing, trying to decipher some meaning from the strange characters, but he failed. He was no closer to knowing what was in them than he had been before he'd jumped into the river.

He had just eased the canister back into its crate when he heard a noise from the direction of the barge. It was the same bang of a door that he'd heard earlier, when Maric and his cronies had come out of the cabin to load the canisters onto the cabin-cruiser. It meant he had just a few seconds to get out of sight. He hurried forward and pulled open the hatchway, crouching low as he exited. In one quick movement he had slipped over the gunwale and into the water, sliding in smoothly to avoid making a splash.

He was just in time; as he clung to the side of the boat, with his eyes and nose just out of the water, it rocked slightly as Maric and his men jumped down into it from the barge. Angus recognised Maric's voice as he spoke to his men.

"Excellent. Now we have the agent, the rest should be easy!"

"Yes, like, ah… shooting the fish in the barrel!"

said one of his men, in what Angus thought was a French accent. Then one of the other thugs spoke.

"Yeah. I wonder how they'll commemorate the 'Testament of the Dead!'" Harsh laughter broke out, echoing unpleasantly from under the road bridge. They were an international bunch, all right; the third voice had sounded English.

"Okay. Let's go," said Maric and there was a low cough and rumble as he started the cabin-cruiser's engine. Realising this was his time to exit, Angus took a deep breath and allowed himself to sink down into the gloomy depths of the river. Looking up through the murky water, he saw the propeller churning up a creamy froth and the boat making a quick turn before disappearing off upstream. Surfacing slowly into the shadow of the barge, he repeated his breathing technique and then began the long underwater swim to the safety of the shadow under the bridge.

★ ★ ★

By the time Angus crawled out of the river, he was freezing cold and shivering violently. He swept the water from his skin using the palms of his hands; the drier he was, the warmer he would feel.

What had felt like a warm evening breeze before, now felt like an icy wind blowing straight off the Arctic tundra.

"Quick, gimme those clothes!" he said, thrusting out his shaking hands, "I'm freezing!"

Danny handed them over.

"So, what did you learn?" he asked, as Angus began pulling on his clothes.

"Not much, the canisters are labelled in Russian, so I've still no idea what's in them. Maric and his neo-Nazi chums made a couple of odd remarks, though. Maric said 'Now we have the agent...' but I didn't see anyone apart from him and his cronies getting into their boat, and one of his pals said something very strange about 'commemorating the Testament of the Dead'. They all found that hilarious."

"Hmm," said Danny. "That probably means it was completely unfunny."

"Yeah, I think you're right. Maybe that's why they hate the Jews so much. There's a great tradition of Jews doing stand-up, but have you ever heard of a Nazi comedian? Maybe they're jealous of the Jews' sense of humour."

Angus chuckled as he threw on his jacket, zipping

it right up to his chin and then thrusting his hands deep into his pockets, clenching and unclenching his fists to get the blood flowing again.

"The trouble is, we still don't know who the agent is or what was in those canisters. More importantly, we have no idea where Maric has gone or what he plans to do next. We seem to have come up against a brick wall. To be honest, I'm too cold and knackered to think about it now. We should head back to the hotel and get some kip, then have another think about it tomorrow."

CHAPTER EIGHT

After breakfast the following morning, Danny and Angus returned to their hotel room and discussed the situation. Neither of them felt particularly optimistic; Maric and his men had disappeared upstream to who-knows-where and they only had a vague idea what might be in the gas canisters that the Russians had given them. The identity of the agent also remained a mystery. All in all, it seemed that the trail had vanished before them.

"Let's not get too downhearted," said Angus, "We do have one lead — if we can discover the meaning of the 'Testament of the Dead', we might be able to work out what they're up to."

"I guess so," replied Danny. "It's a bit of a long shot though, isn't it?"

"Yes, but I've had long shots come off for me before." He paused to think for a moment. "I think I'll fire up the laptop and do some research on the internet."

"What do you want me to do while you're doing that?"

"Hmm. There's not much you can do. Look…" Angus pulled out his wallet. "You've been working pretty hard over the last few days. Here's a fistful of Zlotys. Go and have a day off. Have a wander round Krakow, buy yourself an ice cream and some souvenirs. Take the camera and practice your photography if you like."

"Okay. Anything you want while I'm out?"

"No thanks, just go and enjoy yourself, you've earned it."

"Thanks."

"And try not to get kidnapped, eh?"

"You know me. I'll do my best, but I can't promise anything!"

Danny stepped out of the hotel and into the warm spring sunshine feeling pretty pleased. He had a wodge of money in his back pocket and Angus's Nikon slung over his shoulder. One of the advantages of having a legal guardian with no real interest in money was that he often just handed over whatever he had in his wallet without properly counting it. This time, he had done exceptionally well

— Angus had handed over the equivalent of forty pounds.

He was disappointed with the way things had gone with regard to Maric, but he had to admit he could do with a break from it all. He'd been on the go, almost non-stop, for over two weeks now; he'd skied across a vast mountain plateau, climbed a mountain in the Bavarian Alps, been chased and shot at by Russian gangsters and travelled thousands of kilometres across Europe. Angus was right; he'd earned a day off.

First things first: he'd wander down to the main square, find a shop that sold ice cream and buy himself a sundae the size of Mont Blanc. Then, he'd maybe go up and have a look at the castle. Maybe. Or he might just go and wander round the shops hunting for souvenirs. He wondered if a Swiss Army knife would count as a 'souvenir'. Probably not; it should really be something Polish. He wondered if the Polish Army had good penknives.

It really was a fantastic morning. The sun filtered through the leaves of the roadside trees in a wash of warm, golden light and brought smiles to the faces of the people who sauntered happily by. He could hear the pealing of church bells now, ringing out musically over the rooftops. He realised that it must be Sunday; he'd been on the road so long he'd lost track of which day of the week it was. The sound of the bells reminded him of the call to prayer he had heard echoing metallically from the minarets of the mosques in Morocco. They were different worlds, he reflected, but humanity stayed the same.

He found his ice cream shop, overlooking the main square and the Wieza Ratuszowa, and the sundae he ordered did indeed rival Mont Blanc in stature. Mont Blanc with banana and chocolate sprinkles perhaps, but Mont Blanc nonetheless. He followed this up with a fruit-juice and sat in the sun watching the world go by.

Try as he might, however, he could not stop thinking about Maric and the 'Adler Kommando'. Sighing, he sat back in his chair. The frustrating thing was that he couldn't see how he could find the answers to any of the questions that crowded his mind – he didn't even know where to start. Sucking down the last of his fruit-juice, he got up and began walking in the direction of the castle. He'd better take the opportunity to have a look at it now; he might not get another chance.

★ ★ ★

The castle was every bit as impressive at close range as he'd thought it would be. Walking up a steep, cobbled road, he passed through the main gates and into the castle enclosure. To his left was a complex and ornate Catholic church with impressive stained glass windows and tall, copper spires. To his right was an imposing brick building that had once been barracks; now it contained a ticket office and café.

Buying his ticket, he walked past the church and through another set of gates to find himself in a large medieval courtyard. There were a few tourists about; a young Japanese couple, an elderly man with a beard and a group of school-kids about Danny's age. As he wandered past, one of the kids called out.

"Hi there!" She was blond, as tall as he was and very good-looking; perhaps even as good-looking as Jennifer Campbell. Danny looked around to see who she was talking to; he wasn't used to beautiful girls hailing him out of the blue.

"Um… yes?" he said, painfully aware that he was going red behind the ears.

"You look like you know what you're doing," she said, smiling. She had even white teeth, dimples, blue eyes… Danny could feel his brain starting to shut down.

"Eh?"

"The camera." She pointed at Angus's professional Nikon SLR camera. "You do know how to use it? Or is it just for show?"

"Um... yes. I mean no. Sorry, I mean yes, I do know how to use it!"

"Oh good! Then could you take a picture of my friends and me with my camera?" she handed over a neat little digital compact.

"Of course, no problem."

She ran back to her friends and they grouped together, facing Danny and grinning. He zoomed in to get a nice, tight picture and pressed the button.

"I'll take another shall I? Make sure we get one with everyone's eyes open?"

They laughed at this and he snapped his shot as they did so. Checking the little screen on the back of the camera he saw it was a great photo – they were all laughing and smiling and looking at the camera. He handed the camera back to the girl, who also examined the picture.

"Hey, that's awesome! You do know what you're doing!"

"Thanks. My uncle's a photojournalist and has

given me a few pointers."

"Cool! Are you here on holiday?"

"Yes." He didn't think there was much point in trying to explain that he was actually in Krakow trying to unravel the mystery behind a diabolical plot being perpetrated by neo-Nazi thugs. "My name's Danny, by the way."

"Nice to meet you. Mine's Alison. We…" she indicated her friends with a jerk of the thumb, "are over here from Canada. Where are you from? You sound British."

"I am. From Cumbria in England originally, but now I live in Scotland."

"Have you been into the museum yet?"

"Not yet."

"Neither have we. Do you want to hang out with us?" Alison asked, then she laughed: "We're meant to be on an international mission of peace so it would be pretty appropriate for us to hang out with people from different countries!"

"Yeah, that sounds cool." Danny wondered what Alison had meant by 'an international mission of peace' and was about to ask, but she was already introducing him to her friends. She reeled off a dozen names, but Danny forgot almost all of them immediately. It didn't really matter, he decided, as long as he knew the name of the beautiful blonde!

A couple of hours later, they stood at the gates of the castle, swapping email addresses and saying goodbye. Danny was very impressed by Alison; she was pretty and funny and cool and adventurous. It was a real shame she lived in Canada and not Dunkeld. Just as she turned to go, he remembered the question he had been meaning to ask.

"You said you were here on 'an international mission of peace', what did you mean?"

"Oh, it's a Jewish thing," she said, "You've heard of Auschwitz and Birkenau?"

"I've heard of Auschwitz. It was one of the concentration camps where the Nazis murdered Jews during the Second World War."

"That's right. It's not far from Krakow, about an hour and a half away. Birkenau is another concentration camp, about three kilometres from Auschwitz. In fact, although Auschwitz is more famous, more people were murdered at Birkenau. On Tuesday, Jews from all over the world will be at Auschwitz and Birkenau commemorating all the people who died there and calling on the world to make sure nothing like that ever happens again." She smiled a little sadly. "My grandfather was one of the few survivors of the camps."

"So you're here for this commemoration thing?"

"Yes, we walk the three kilometres between the two camps along an old railway track which the Nazis used to take people from Auschwitz to Birkenau for extermination. When we reach Birkenau, holocaust survivors tell stories from their time in the camps. It's called The Testament of Survivors."

As the significance of Alison's words sank in, Danny's face went as white as a funeral shroud. It was as though the blood in his veins had suddenly gone cold. An awful crawling sensation shivered across the skin of his arms and up the back of his neck. The Testament of Survivors. It was too much of a coincidence: neo-Nazis, some kind of lethal gas, thousands of Jews in one place – suddenly The Testament of the Dead made terrible, appalling sense.

"Are you okay?" Alison was looking at him curiously.

"Yes, sorry!" Danny pulled himself together with an

effort. "I just realised, I'm really late for something...
I've got to go! I'm going to be in big trouble!"

Danny burst into their hotel room; he was breathing
hard from running, but still managed to blurt out
his news:

"I know what the Adler Kommando are planning!"

Angus looked up from his laptop in surprise.

"How on earth...?"

"It's a long story... but I think they are planning
a terrorist attack. There is a commemoration event
being held at the old Auschwitz concentration camp
on Tuesday. There will be loads of Jewish people
there – it's called 'The Testament of Survivors'! Those
canisters with the skull and crossbones on them;
I think they must be poison gas or something."

Angus stared at Danny in horror. "How do you
know this?" he asked.

So Danny told him how he'd met Alison and her
friends at the castle and how she had mentioned
'The Testament of Survivors'.

"As soon as she said it, everything just seemed so
obvious," he finished.

"This is awful," said Angus "But it's a good thing you ran into that girl. I couldn't find anything on the internet about a Testament of the Dead that could possibly be connected to what Maric has been doing. If you hadn't spoken to her we still wouldn't have a clue as to what he is up to."

"So you think I might be right?"

"It makes sense, doesn't it? Neo-Nazis…" He paused, frowning — then stared wide-eyed at Danny. "Of course! How could I be so stupid! The agent isn't a person!"

"What is it then?"

But Angus didn't answer. He had turned back towards his laptop and was thumping away at the keyboard. Danny saw a search engine pop up on screen, swiftly followed by a page of results. Angus clicked on one.

"Look, 'poison gas agent'. It's from an online encyclopaedia."

The page described various types of poison gas. Halfway down was a heading – 'Nerve Agents'. Peering over Angus's shoulder, Danny read the description.

Nerve Agents attack the central nervous system, making the victim's muscles go into spasm. This includes the muscles that control breathing, and the victim slowly suffocates. Nerve Agents are the most dangerous of all chemical weapons.

"So you think that's what is in those canisters?"

"I'd bet my life on it!"

"But how did the Russian gangsters get their hands on it?"

"I'd guess that it has been stolen from a decommissioning programme."

"What's that?"

"A lot of countries, including the Russian Federation, hold a supply of chemical weapons, usually left over from the twentieth century. However, most nations accept that nerve agents and the like are pretty nasty and often agree to destroy some of their stockpile as part of a peace treaty."

"Isn't that a good thing?"

"Sure. Decommissioning generally makes the world a safer place."

"But...?"

"But unfortunately the weapons don't always get

destroyed. Sometimes a corrupt official or soldier spirits some of it away and sells it to the highest bidder. And because it is assumed that the weapons have been destroyed in the programme..."

"Let me guess, nobody ever notices they are missing..."

"Exactly."

"But that's madness!"

"Aye."

They fell into silence for a moment, each lost in their thoughts; Angus seeing the big picture — the thousands of innocent people who could be killed; Danny taking it more personally, thinking about the girl and her friends who he'd met that afternoon.

"We've got to do something," he said, looking at Angus.

"Of course. Doing something is what we do."

CHAPTER NINE

By the time they arrived in the small industrial town of Oświęcim, the location of the Auschwitz and Birkenau camps, it was late and darkness had fallen. Deciding that poking around the camp in the dark would be a waste of time, they found a nearby hotel and settled in for the night. It was, as Angus said, a 'filthy hovel' and nowhere near as nice as the hotel they'd been staying at in Krakow. However, it was close to the former concentration camp and they were too tired to look for a better place.

Their room had a tiny, greasy window with a back-alley view and was decorated with psychedelic floral wallpaper. The ceiling was stained brown with decades of cigarette smoke and the lumpy beds were covered with orange and brown nylon sheets. When Danny suggested it was the kind of place you'd go if you were on the run from the police, Angus did not disagree.

After going over what they had already learned, Danny said, "How are we going to stop them, Angus? Shouldn't we be telling the police?"

"Of course we should. Unfortunately, we don't have any real evidence that the attack is going to happen. Sure, we could tell them everything we've seen and done, but when you think about it, it all sounds pretty far-fetched. I mean: stolen Nazi art, Russian gangsters, secret exchanges on the Vistula... I think we'd be lucky not to be locked in the nearest loony bin."

"So what can we do?"

"We need to have a close look at the Auschwitz and Birkenau camps and see if we can find any hard evidence of what the Adler Kommando are up to. If we can do that, then we should be able to persuade the police to act; perhaps convince them to cancel the event and do a thorough search of the area."

The following morning Danny and Angus walked the short distance to Auschwitz concentration camp along a straight, tree-lined road. The sun was shining weakly through a morning mist that clung like silver gossamer to the trees and buildings. It was cold, but the sunshine promised a fine, warm spring day.

"I've heard the birds don't sing at Auschwitz,"

said Danny.

"Hmm. Sounds like a myth," replied Angus. "Animals aren't affected by the horrors of humanity."

"You are probably right. Still, I don't hear any birdsong, do you?"

"No," Angus conceded.

Danny was surprised by the camp's location; he had expected it to be hidden out in the middle of nowhere, far away from inquisitive eyes. But here it was, right on the edge of town, just across the road from people's homes; as though it was just another respectable industrial facility. Then he realised that this was exactly what he was looking at: an industrial facility for the efficient murder of human beings. Suddenly, he felt sick and light-headed. The terrible reality of the place had hit him abruptly and unexpectedly. What made it worse, was the conviction that Maric was planning to kill yet more people here tomorrow.

"You alright?" asked Angus, looking at him with concern.

"Yeah, let's just get on with it, eh?"

The camp, now a museum, had been preserved almost exactly as it had been at the end of the war. They entered through the wrought iron gates which bore the infamous legend "Arbacht Macht Frei". It had been a lie, of course: work had never set free any of those who had entered the camp.

They found a compound closely packed with tall brick buildings and low wooden huts. It was difficult to know where to start.

"Okay, let's do this intelligently!" said Angus. "We can't search the whole camp, so we need to think about the most likely places for the gas to be. Where would *you* put the stuff if you were a homicidal maniac?"

"I don't know." Danny was a bright kid, but thinking like a murderous lunatic was beyond him. A part of him was quite glad of it.

"You'd put it where it would kill the most people," said Angus.

"I suppose so."

"Right, so setting it off between the two camps, while people are walking between them, would be pointless. Some people will be walking fast, some slowly and the line of people will be stretched out over a large distance. Set off your poison gas somewhere on the route and you only kill whoever happens to be near it at that moment."

Danny was beginning to understand.

"So, you set it off at the start, when everyone is waiting to set off, or at the end, where everyone gathers to listen to the survivors tell their stories," he said.

"Exactly!"

"Still, that doesn't narrow it down much. The gas could still be hidden in any of the buildings in Auschwitz or Birkenau. That's a lot of buildings and a lot of them are closed to the public, so we wouldn't be able to get in to search them."

"No, I suppose you are right."

"Wait a minute, though..." said Danny, "Do you have the map of Poland with you?"

"I think so... pretty sure I threw it in here with the guidebook this morning." Angus reached into his day-pack and rummaged around for a moment before pulling it out. "Here we go!"

Danny took it from him eagerly and unfolded it. Finding the area around Krakow and Oświęcim, he studied it intently for a few moments then broke into a wide grin.

"I reckon I might be able to narrow down our search quite a lot!"

"Really, how?"

"Maric picked up the gas canisters in a boat, right?

I reckon there has to be a reason for that. I think he was planning to transport it here up the river. Remember how he disappeared off upstream after the exchange? Look at the map…" he turned it so Angus could see. "If you follow the Vistula upstream from Krakow you come to Oświęcim! And this branch of the river…" he pointed to a tributary stream that joined the Vistula from the South, "comes right past Auschwitz!"

"Holy cow! Danny — you are absolutely right!"

"But," continued Danny, "while the river goes right past Auschwitz, Birkenau is three kilometres away. Those canisters looked heavy. I reckon that Maric and his pals wouldn't want to carry them further than was totally necessary; which means that the most likely place for them to have hidden them is in Auschwitz."

Angus slapped Danny on the back with a thump that nearly knocked him off his feet.

"Well done! Excellent thinking! I think we should head down to the river and see if there is any evidence that Maric has unloaded the canisters there. You never know, they might have even left the boat there!"

★ ★ ★

Maric had not left the boat by the riverbank. That would have been too convenient. In fact, at first glance, there appeared to be nowhere that the Adler Kommando could have unloaded their deadly cargo. There were no jetties, slipways or landing wharfs; just weeds, bushes and low muddy banks. Nevertheless, they walked slowly down the westerly bank, searching hopefully for some clue that would confirm Danny's idea.

The theory did seem to be quite plausible — the river passed within a hundred metres of the wire that surrounded Auschwitz. If the Adler Kommando had brought the canisters up the river, they would only have had to carry them a short distance to get them to the camp. And there were no houses in the immediate vicinity. If they had come at night, no-one would have noticed what they were up to.

Eventually, at a point where the river began to curve away from the camp, Angus stopped and pointed to a spot on the riverbank a few yards ahead.

"See where the grass has that silvery sheen?"

"Yes."

"That's where the flattened stalks are reflecting the sun. It means someone has passed that way. By the width of the path, I'd say several people, or one person making a number of trips. Let's go and take a look."

Reaching the spot they saw it had been the scene of quite a lot of activity. At the edge of the river, a shallow bank of mud rose out of the water, to meet a tangle of weeds on the edge of the grassy riverbank. The mud was criss-crossed with footprints and the grass was heavily trampled. Angus stooped to examine the mud.

"Three men," he said. "All quite big guys, going by the shoe-size. All wearing heavy boots. Hmm…" He paused for a moment. "Look at the depth of the footprints. They are a little bit deeper than mine and I'm no featherweight. That could mean they were carrying something heavy. The short length of the stride also suggests that." He followed the trail of footprints up the muddy bank to the weeds. "Here—" he pointed to some leaves that had been crushed by the passing feet. "See the bruises on these leaves? They are still quite dark, that means these tracks are reasonably fresh. Probably left in the early hours of this morning."

"Cool," said Danny. "How do you know all this stuff?"

"I wrote a piece on the Wildlife Protection Unit of the Kenyan Wildlife Service. They showed me a few things about tracking."

"Useful."

"It has been... more than once."

Angus stepped up onto the grass, keeping the trail of footprints between himself and the sun — they would be easier to see that way. The trail headed straight in the direction of the Auschwitz perimeter fence. He followed it slowly, looking ahead for signs that would tell him where the men had gone — a crushed leaf, a broken twig, a partial footprint in a patch of mud. All the signs led in the same direction: towards one particular point in the fence.

When they reached it, what they saw came as no surprise. A hole had been cut in the fence, low to the ground, and then the wire had been pushed back into position. It was crudely done, but that didn't matter — it would not be noticed by anyone who wasn't looking for it.

"Come on," he said, pulling back the wire. Danny

fell to his hands and knees and wriggled through, swiftly followed by his uncle. On the other side, they picked up the trail again, following it over an area of muddy grass. After a few paces, Angus pointed at the ground.

"Look at this!" There were several large, rectangular impressions on the grass. "These marks are about the same size as the crates I saw on the boat; the ones the canisters had been stored in."

"They must have put the crates down here to rest," said Danny. "I reckon these marks have to have been made by the Adler Kommando!"

"There's no doubt in my mind," replied Angus.

A few metres further on, however, their luck ran out. They came to a hard gravel path and, try as he might, Angus could not see where the trail led. They were back in the main compound of Auschwitz, surrounded again by dozens of buildings, in any one of which the gas might lie hidden. Danny was severely disappointed.

"Damn it! I thought the trail was going to lead us straight to the gas!"

"Yes, me too," said Angus. "Still, at least we know one thing for sure. The Adler Kommando definitely brought the canisters up the river and then sneaked them into Auschwitz through the wire. We may not know where they are in Auschwitz, but we do know that they are here and not in Birkenau. That reduces the search area quite a lot."

"But there are still too many places here to search. Not to mention the fact we can't get into a lot of them!"

"That's true," said Angus. "I think it's time we called in the police. We'll just have to do our best to convince them we're not making the whole thing up!"

Inspektor Borkowski of the Oświęcim Police Department gazed unblinkingly at Angus with a mixture of tired cynicism and frank disbelief. He was a balding man in his late forties, with heavy eyelids and full, sneering lips. Perched on the end of his nose sat a pair of steel framed spectacles which seemed to be positioned for peering over, rather than through. His face could have been purpose-built for delivering looks of withering contempt.

Angus had to admit it, though, their story did seem

pretty far-fetched. They had very little evidence, mostly just things they'd seen or overheard, often in situations where Angus or Danny had been the ones breaking the law.

"So," Borkowski said when Angus had finished telling their story. "I am expected to believe that some neo-Nazis are planning to gas the Testament of Survivors tomorrow? With a deadly nerve agent, no less! The evidence you have for this? Nothing. You cannot even say for sure what was in those canisters – just that they had a skull and cross-bones on them. It could have been anything! I am simply expected to agree with your wild theory and order the cancellation of the event!" He laughed — a brief snort of derision.

"I can show you the footprints in the mud, if you like, and the hole in the fence. Why would anyone else want break into an old concentration camp?" said Angus.

"You could have made these marks, as part of some stupid joke. Perhaps it is you who I should throw in prison? You have already admitted to breaking into this man's house and setting his car on fire!"

"But…"

"Mr. McKinlay, stop! My officers searched the

camp yesterday. Do you think we are not aware of right wing extremists? Do you think we are stupid and incompetent? If there had been anything to find, my officers would have found it!"

"The tracks on the riverbank suggest the gas was brought ashore last night – *after* your officers searched the camp!"

"So you say, Mr McKinlay. You know this from tracking lions in the African bush!" Borkowski smiled, a lopsided sneer that left them in no doubt as to what he thought of Angus's tracking skills.

"Why won't you believe me? Thousands of people could die tomorrow…"

Borkowski's fist crashed down on to his desk, cutting Angus off mid-sentence. His anger sizzled in the air like a tangible thing; showing clearly in the white of his knuckles and the hard glitter of his eyes.

"Enough! Mr McKinlay, I have better things to do than listen to the crazed ramblings of a convicted criminal!"

"What? I'm no criminal!"

"I'm not stupid, Mr McKinlay. While you were waiting in the reception area, I did a little checking. Your criminal record makes interesting reading…"

Danny stared in wonder at his uncle, who had gone

red in the face and looked genuinely bemused.

"I haven't a clue what you are talking about!" said Angus, angrily.

Borkowski lifted some sheets of paper from his desk and peered at them through his glasses.

"It is an impressively long list of offences!"

"Rubbish! I told you, I'm not a criminal!"

Ignoring him, the policeman began to read.

"Breaking and entering."

"That does sound like Angus," muttered Danny under his breath.

"Theft of a motor vehicle."

Sudden realisation spread over Angus's face.

"Oh… wait a minute… You are talking about Albania."

"Dangerous driving."

"Yes, definitely Albania."

"Theft of a second motor vehicle."

"Yeah, those Albanian cars don't go round corners too well."

"Failing to stop for a police officer."

"He was shooting at me!"

"Assault of a police officer with a deadly weapon!"

"Like I say, he was shooting at me. And I don't think throwing a cabbage at someone qualifies as assault with a deadly weapon…"

"Resisting arrest, attempted escape from police custody… The list goes on! You were sentenced to six months in prison for your crimes. It was only the strenuous efforts of your embassy that got you released after three weeks! Why they bothered I have no idea!"

Angus took a step forward and placed his hands flat on Borkowski's desk.

"They bothered because I told them exactly what I had been doing! I was investigating mafia corruption in the Albanian Police Force. The policeman I was investigating was the one who shot at me. He was as guilty as hell – everybody knew it – we just couldn't prove it. The Albanian Government ordered my immediate release to keep me quiet and to avoid an international incident."

"That is your story. Now, tell me, should I believe you – or the INTERPOL file I have in front of me? It makes no mention of police corruption…"

It was going badly, Angus could sense the boiling rage in Borkowski's voice. They were moments from being thrown out onto the street.

"INTERPOL?" Danny interrupted suddenly. "Would you believe the word of a senior police officer who works with INTERPOL? A Chief Inspector with Special Branch of the Metropolitan Police in London?"

"I expect so," said Borkowski grudgingly, his eyes narrowing with suspicion.

"Good. Then give Chief Inspector Newby at New Scotland Yard a call. He will vouch for us. I have his number right here…" He reached into his pocket for his phone.

"Don't bother!" said Borkowski. "I will find it for myself!"

The office was suddenly quiet, except for the staccato clatter of inexpert typing, as the policeman looked up Newby's phone number on his computer. Moments later he was thumping it into the phone on his desk.

"Hello? Hello? Ah, yes. This is Inspektor Borkowski of Oświęcim Police Department… Oświęcim… Poland…"

A few minutes later, Borkowski replaced the handset of his phone and regarded the pair with a baleful glare. He looked like he might be considering the manner of their execution. At last, he broke the silence.

"Well, Chief Inspector Newby certainly seems to think you are reliable. Of course, there is no guarantee he has not been duped by you in some way…"

He paused for a moment.

"I'll be frank, Mr McKinlay. I do not like you. I do not trust you. If it were not for the conversation I have just had with Chief Inspector Newby, I would simply throw you out on the street. Or maybe even into jail, for wasting police time. As it is, I am willing to come to a compromise. I will not order the cancelation of the event on the say-so of a convicted criminal, but I will order another search of the camp."

The offer was so grudging that Danny and Angus realised this was as good as it was going to get and they spoke in unison.

"Thank you!"

Borkowski held up his hand to stop them.

"However, you may have seen in the news that the US President is currently on a tour of Central Europe. He will be in Krakow for three and a half hours tomorrow morning. Every policeman for miles around has been drafted in to help with security. That includes all of the officers under my command. Nonetheless, I will see what I can do."

Turning in his chair, the policeman picked up his phone again and stabbed in a number. There followed a long conversation in Polish with someone unknown. At last, with what sounded like a grunt of agreement, Borkowski tossed the phone back on to its cradle and stood up.

"I have spoken to a friend of mine in Krakow. He has said he will send an officer tomorrow morning who will help look for this poison gas of yours."

"One officer!" Angus exclaimed. "One officer! What good is that going to do!"

Borkowski was unapologetic.

"Officer Silberstein will come up the river by police patrol boat. She will arrive at 7 am tomorrow morning."

"7 am! You're not serious? That's two hours before the event is due to start!"

"Enough!" Borkowski slammed his desk with the palm of his hand. "I have done all I can! Now get out of my office before I throw you in jail!"

Outside in the street, Danny looked to Angus for reassurance.

"Do you think it's going to work out? Two hours to search the whole of Auschwitz doesn't seem like a very long time. And what if we do find the canisters? Do we have a go at disarming them?"

"I don't know. I really don't," said Angus. For the first time in his life, Danny saw defeat in the eyes of his uncle. His uncle — who had faced untold terrors in the most remote corners of the globe, who had risked his life countless times to break stories of corruption, greed and violence. His fearless, tenacious, bullet-proof uncle.

This time it was different, Danny recognised that. It wasn't just Angus's life on the line; it was the lives of thousands of men, women and children. It was clear he felt the responsibility acutely, all the more so because it seemed that he could do nothing to avert the coming disaster. Belatedly, Angus realised that Danny was looking at him. Forcing a smile he put a hand on Danny's shoulder.

"I expect we'll find a way. Maybe this Officer Silberstein will turn out to be some sort of bomb-finding genius!"

"I hope so!"

"Me too, because it seems like it's up to the three of us to find the gas!"

CHAPTER TEN

7 am on Tuesday morning was cold and damp. Yesterday's sun had disappeared behind a thick blanket of grey cloud and a heavy dew had fallen, soaking everything. A silver mantle of droplets covered the grass of the riverbank and crystal beads of water hung in long lines from the rusting barbed-wire that surrounded the camp – as though patiently queuing to fall from its rusting points.

Alison would just be getting up, Danny supposed. Perhaps, at this very moment, she was looking out of the window at the leaden sky and wondering what the day would hold. By no stretch of the imagination could she guess the possibilities. No flight of fancy would ever suggest to her that her life depended on a boy and his uncle who waited on a grim riverbank in the grey light of dawn.

They heard the motorboat a few moments before they saw it; a deep, thrumming drone disturbing the morning hush. Then it appeared from round the bend, about a hundred metres downstream — a small river patrol boat, with a tiny cabin and a huge outboard engine. It was travelling very fast, throwing up twin arcs of spray from its bows and leaving a thick white trail of foam behind it. As it neared the spot where Danny and Angus stood, it turned, the engine note dropped suddenly and then cut out altogether. As it thumped into the bank, the cabin door opened and a head popped out. "Hallo? You are Mr. McKinlay?"

"Yes," Angus snapped. "You must be Silberstein." She nodded. "Quick, we've no time to lose. There are only three of us to search the whole of Auschwitz. You may not believe our story, but…."

Silberstein held up her hand to stop him.

"Don't worry. I believe you! I was only told your story when I came on shift this morning. If I had known earlier I would have come as soon as I heard! It happens I have come across the Adler Kommando before. I had to police one of their rallies once. They are filled with hate for everyone who is not like them — I would believe anything of them!"

"Well, that's something. Still, we have to get moving. Like I said, there are just three of us to search the whole camp. I'm afraid I don't fancy our chances of finding the gas in time."

Unexpectedly, Silberstein smiled.

"Actually," she said, as she jumped down from the boat, her boots sinking ankle deep into the mud, "there are four of us... HUGO!"

There was a sudden scrabbling inside the boat, followed by a yelp. A moment later a fuzzy, black and white head appeared in its bows. In a single bound, Hugo cleared the gunwale and landed on the grass in front of Danny.

"You brought your dog," said Angus flatly. He did not seem impressed.

"He is not *my* dog. He belongs to the Police Department," said Silberstein. "I am his handler — Hugo is trained to find explosives."

"How will that help? We are looking for poison gas, not explosives."

"That is correct. However, to spread the gas over a wide area, the Adler Kommando will blow it up using a conventional explosive. Almost certainly Semtex or C4. If Hugo can find the explosive then... well, then we have found the gas also."

"Um, I don't want to be rude..." said Danny, peering intently into the dog's face as he scratched him behind both ears, "but is Hugo a bit cross-eyed?"

Silberstein flushed.

"He does not smell with his eyes. His sense of smell

is many thousands of times better than ours and he is more likely than any of us to find the gas!"

Danny realised he had touched a nerve and decided not to ask about Hugo's chronic drooling. Angus took another look at the dog, reassessing his impression of it. It was a black and white Cocker Spaniel, perhaps a bit thick around the midriff, but brimming with health and energy. It didn't look much like a highly trained sniffer dog to him, but then, he wasn't exactly sure what a highly trained sniffer dog was meant to look like.

Could this chubby, cross-eyed little spaniel really be the answer to finding the poison gas before the Adler Kommando could set it off? Hugo, oblivious to Angus's critical eye, was wagging his entire hindquarters enthusiastically and depositing copious quantities of saliva onto Danny's trainers. Sighing, Angus realised that Silberstein was right — the dog really was their only hope. If Hugo could not find the gas, then a lot of people were going to die.

"Come on then," he said, "I'll show you where they brought the canisters ashore."

The trail was less distinct than it had been the day before, but it was still there. They could still see footprints in the mud of the river bank and the broken blades of grass pointing towards the hole in the fence. Inside the camp, they showed Silberstein the rectangular impressions that had been left in the grass. Hugo sniffed the area curiously for a few seconds, but then appeared to lose interest, wandering off in the direction of a nearby telegraph pole.

"Hugo!" Silberstein called. Looking round, he stood for a moment staring at her, as though he was trying to remember who she was.

"Hugo!"

He turned and trotted back.

"He's not going to keep doing that is he?" asked Angus.

"Doing what?"

"Wandering off."

"No. He is an excellent dog. You wait and see." Silberstein was going red in the face again.

"Okay. It's just…"

"I am aware of the gravity of the situation, Mr. McKinlay. I am not blind." She nodded in the direction of a squat concrete building close to the front gate of the camp. A small group of people were setting up a long table and chairs while a few others were carefully unloading some loud-speakers from a battered Volkswagen van.

The preparations for the Testament of Survivors had begun. It would not be long before a crowd of thousands filled the area in which they now stood. Somewhere, hidden amongst these relics of the holocaust, lurked a device that could end all of their lives. Silberstein could feel her stomach tighten and her heart begin to pound. It was all down to her now — her and Hugo. She did not dare tell Angus that Hugo would only be able to find the bomb if the Adler Kommando had used C4 as their explosive. Semtex was almost impossible to detect by its smell alone, even for as talented a nose as Hugo's.

She called him over and gestured again at the flattened grass where the crates had been. Hugo sniffed the ground once more. He looked up at Silberstein as if to say "So?" then back at the ground.

"Come on, Hugo! Anything here?"

Hugo looked at the grass and then back at Silberstein.

"Look," said Angus, impatiently "We can't muck

around here all day…"

Suddenly Hugo's head tilted slightly and his ears cocked forward. It was an almost imperceptible movement but Silberstein knew immediately what it meant.

"Shh!" She held up her hand for silence. "He has something."

Hugo trotted slowly towards a smaller patch of flattened grass a few metres from where they stood. The closer he got, the faster he moved and by the time he had reached his destination he was moving in quick zigzags, his nose an inch from the ground. Circling the spot, he snuffled eagerly through the grass and let out a brief, excited whimper. He then sat down and looked up at Silberstein. It seemed the Adler Kommando had used C4.

"Yes! He has found traces of explosive! Good boy! They may have put a bag down here that held the explosive. Good boy, Hugo!" Silberstein reached into a pocket and pulled out a biscuit, which she tossed to him. "Okay Hugo, let's find the bomb!"

They set off at a brisk walk for the nearest hut, a building that appeared to be in use as an office. Peering through a window, they could see a comfortably proportioned lady in a woollen suit typing away at a computer and a young man standing next to a photocopier with a bored look on his face. Silberstein rapped the door once with her knuckles and entered, saying something in Polish as she strode purposefully into the room.

The woman nodded and the young man glanced over, but neither took much interest. Danny guessed she had told them it was some kind of routine security check.

Guiding Hugo through the room, Silberstein concentrated on larger cupboards and a store room at the far end, but nothing piqued the slightest interest in the spaniel. In just a few minutes they were back outside and heading for the next hut.

"I'll say this for him," said Angus, "he works fast!"

It was true, Hugo had searched the hut in a fraction of the time it would have taken the three humans, who would have had to rely on visually inspecting every last place that the poison gas could have been hidden. That would have meant opening every cupboard, crate or storage space in every building in Auschwitz — a task that would have taken hours, if not days. But if Hugo could search each building in a matter of a few minutes, they had a much better chance of finding the gas in time.

The next hut was clearly used for storage and was filled with cardboard boxes and large wooden crates. A couple of sit-upon lawn mowers stood in one corner along with some other gardening equipment. There was nobody about, but the door had been left wide open. It took a little longer to search this hut than the previous one, as there were more places in which canisters could be hidden, but again Hugo found nothing. Angus glanced at his watch.

"It's nearly eight o'clock. Maric won't set off the bomb until around nine, to be sure of killing the maximum number of people. That gives us an hour. I hope it's going to be long enough."

"It will be long enough," said Silberstein with a confidence she did not feel. "Hugo will find the bomb."

They ran to the next hut in line to find its windows boarded up and door secured with a heavy brass padlock.

"Perhaps we could save some time by not searching this one?" said Danny. "It doesn't look as if anyone has been inside for years."

The building was covered with a thick layer of grime and cobwebs and the screws that held the window boards in place were brown with rust.

A thick crop of weeds grew in a clump beneath a drainpipe at one corner of the hut, adding to the air of abandonment.

"This doesn't look like it's been tampered with either," he added, lifting up the padlock to examine it.

"No," said Silberstein, with a raised eyebrow. "In fact, it looks brand new. Which is strange when you see how old and rusty the rest of the hut is. Wait a minute…" Striding quickly over to the drainpipe at the corner of the hut, she bent over and started searching through the tangle of weeds below. A few seconds later she straightened and, with a grim smile on her lips, threw something to Danny. Putting his hands out to catch it, he felt something hard and heavy hit his palm. It was a brass padlock not unlike the one hanging from the door of the hut, only the shackle of this padlock had been cut neatly in two.

"Probably cut with an ordinary set of bolt-cutters," said Silberstein. "A new one was then put in its place to make it seem like no-one had been inside. The fact that no-one here would have the key to the new lock would also delay anybody who decided to search the hut before the event. I will be very surprised if the bomb is not in this hut!"

"Another task for the Raffles Kit?" said Danny, looking up at his uncle.

"Well, it would be, if I'd thought to bring it with me!" said Angus. "Never mind, I'll just have to use the Raffles Shoulder instead." Danny barely had time to look puzzled before Angus had backed off a few paces and then hurled himself at the door like a human wrecking ball.

BANG!

As he slammed into it, the door buckled, splintered and then tore from its hinges. Angus, no longer in control of his own momentum, carried on into the hut, where he fell with a crash into a pile of old tarpaulins and tins of paint. There was a final clatter and grunt as a stepladder toppled on to the pile.

"Cool!" said Danny, from the doorway. "Not very dignified, but quite cool!"

Angus laughed, threw off the stepladder and staggered to his feet.

"One day, grasshopper, I shall teach you the secrets of the Raffles Shoulder — and you too will be able to pass through doors as if by magic."

"Just one thing: how did you know it wouldn't be booby-trapped?"

"Ah, well…" Angus hesitated and went a little red

in the face.

"Come on!" interrupted Silberstein, getting impatient with what she saw as tomfoolery. "We have a bomb to find, remember?"

They could see that searching this hut would be a difficult task. There were boxes and crates piled up in angular mountains; wardrobes, filing cabinets, and rolled up carpets. If you were looking for a place to hide something, this was about as good a place as can be imagined. What's more, only two of the lights worked — and with the windows boarded up this made the hut a very gloomy place indeed.

Silberstein began a systematic search immediately, directing Hugo to a pile of wooden crates to their left. Once these had been searched, they moved on to a dusty wardrobe behind. In this manner they progressed down the length of the hut, searching all the possible hiding places to the left of the doorway. When they reached the far end, they turned round and began a search of the right side of the hut. Despite the number of potential hiding places, they had returned to the doorway in less than ten minutes.

"I can't understand it," said Silberstein. "I would have bet a month's pay that the bomb would be in this hut. That broken padlock seemed like very good evidence, but Hugo has found nothing."

"I must admit," said Angus, "the padlock was mightily suspicious. Are you sure that Hugo would definitely find the bomb if it was here? Could they have masked the smell somehow?"

"No, if the bomb was here, Hugo would have found it. I am sure of it."

They stared at each other for a moment, uncertain of what to do next.

"Well, I suppose we'd better have a look at the next hut," said Angus, turning to leave.

"What about the attic?" said Danny.

Angus's head snapped round.

"What attic?"

"That one." Danny pointed to the far end of the hut where, just visible through the gloom, a small hatchway could be seen in the ceiling.

"Should we have a look up there? Just in case? I know where we can find a stepladder."

Once they had erected the stepladder under the hatchway, Angus climbed up and pushed it open. Taking his little key-ring torch from his pocket, he flicked it on and peered into the dark void of the attic.

"More junk," he reported. "Mostly boxes of files... probably worth checking out though. Come on then... pass him up."

Silberstein lifted Hugo carefully, passing him into Angus's waiting arms. Angus then pushed the dog up into the attic. Hugo, pausing only to lick Angus's face, scrambled up into the loft and started snuffling around. Almost immediately, there came that familiar brief whimper, followed by a hurried scrabbling sound — then silence. Angus turned his torch back on and sent the beam in Hugo's direction. At the far end of the attic, Hugo was sitting motionless next to a tall pile of cardboard boxes and staring straight into Angus's eyes.

"I think," said Angus quietly, "we have found our bomb."

By the time all of them had squeezed into the attic, it seemed like a very small space indeed. The only light came from Angus's key-ring torch; a tiny flare of yellow light in a cramped grotto of black shadows, dust and cobwebs. Before them were stacked around two dozen cardboard boxes forming a high wall, past which they could not see. Behind this wall, it seemed, lay the poison gas they had been hunting for.

"I wonder if its booby trapped," said Silberstein, remembering Danny's earlier comment.

"Only one way to find out," said Angus, taking hold of a box at the top of the pile and pulling it towards him. Nothing happened.

"I guess not." He smiled, both Silberstein and Danny looked like ghosts in the pale light of the torch. The stress was etched clearly into both of their faces; neither of them were used to tension as acute as this. Angus decided not to shout "BANG!" as he pulled down the second box. The joke would probably get him lynched.

Soon, Angus had pulled down enough boxes and could see what lay beyond. Retrieving his torch from Danny, who had been holding it while he dismantled the wall, he shone the beam into the opening.

"Aye. We've found it all right. Come and take a look."

Silberstein and Danny crowded forward to peer through the hole. On the other side, in its dark and secret hiding place, sat the most sinister thing

Danny had ever seen. Three metal crates — each crate holding six green cylinders. Cylinders marked with the skull and crossbones in red, white and black. The crates had been arranged around an object that, even to Danny's untrained eye, could only be a bomb. It consisted of a large rectangular packet with a black plastic box fixed to its side.

The three of them stood and stared for a moment, unable to think of what to do next. Even though he had seen all the evidence and had known exactly what to expect, it came as a terrible shock to Danny to come face to face with the reality of the Adler Kommando's plot. It had all seemed so diabolical, so absurdly evil, that he would not have been surprised if it had turned out that he and Angus had imagined the whole thing.

"What are we going to do?" he whispered, as though talking normally might set the device off.

Angus glanced at his watch.

"Hmm. Eight thirty. How long before a bomb disposal team can get here?"

Silberstein bit her bottom lip.

"Too long. We only have one bomb disposal unit and it is based in Warsaw. It will probably be in Krakow today, for the visit of the US president, but

Krakow is still over an hour away."

"Can we call in some police officers to clear the camp?"

"Every police officer for miles around will be in Krakow. The timing is terrible…"

There was a lingering, uncomfortable silence. Danny became aware of how hot and stuffy it was in the attic. There was no sound, save the noise of his breathing. No movement of air at all. How could it be so dark in here, when it was broad daylight outside? Was he imagining it, or was he finding it more difficult to breathe than normal? He took a deep breath. It really was hot in here! A wave of nausea swept over him and he felt suddenly like he was about to suffocate. What if the poison gas was already leaking from one of the cylinders? What was it the encyclopaedia had said? *Nerve Agents attack the central nervous system, making the victim's muscles go into spasm. This includes the muscles that control breathing, and the victim slowly suffocates…*

He nearly snapped — nearly panicked. Nearly ran headlong for the hatchway — to breathe fresh air again.

"You alright lad?"

Danny shuddered.

"Sorry. Just the claustrophobia. It creeps up on me."

"You are doing just fine."

"Um, Mr McKinlay… I have some more bad news!" Silberstein said, peering closely at the sinister cluster of cylinders in their metal cage. "This is not just any poison gas. This is VX!"

"What on earth is VX?"

Silberstein pointed at the Cyrillic writing that had baffled Angus when he had climbed aboard Maric's cabin-cruiser three nights before.

"VX is the most deadly nerve agent ever made! If this bomb goes off we are all dead. Me, you, Danny and everyone here for the Testament of Survivors. In fact, it will kill everyone within a mile of here!"

Danny felt Angus's hand grip his shoulder.

"Danny, I need you to do something for me."

"Okay."

"Go and get me an event official. Just grab the nearest person in a fluorescent vest and bring them here. We need to try and evacuate the camp – with or without the help of the police. If this VX stuff is as bad as Silberstein says it might be pointless, but we have to try!"

Danny hesitated for a second, dumbfounded by the horror of the moment. Everybody within a mile…

But it was a brief instant of indecisiveness — seconds later he was crashing down the stepladder and sprinting from the hut. Outside, he ran across the concrete and into the crowd. There were thousands here now, a vast throng of people — men, women and children. Fathers, mothers, brothers and sisters.

He soon found what he was looking for – a man in fluorescent yellow vest.

"Hey! Excuse me! Do you speak English?"

The man smiled apologetically, then shook his head.

"You need to come with me!" Danny persisted, grabbing the man by his arm and pulling him towards the hut. "This way! Come on!"

The man resisted, a look of irritation on his face. He said something in Polish.

"This way! Police! Poison gas!" Danny was desperate now, trying to convey the urgency of the situation through his manner. He looked at the man with pleading eyes. "Come on!"

The man shrugged him off.

"English- no!" he said.

Danny searched around for someone else; someone younger, perhaps more likely to speak English. He spotted a slight young man about thirty metres away and wriggled through the crowd towards him.

"Hey, do you speak English?" he shouted.

The young man turned and shrugged.

"English? No."

Danny felt like screaming. He'd met plenty of Poles who spoke English well. Where on earth were they now? He sized the young man up, wondering if he would be able to physically drag him to the hut and push him up in to the attic.

At that moment he caught a fleeting glimpse of blonde hair amongst the crowd. There it was again! Between the shoulders of surrounding adults, he could just make out a head of golden curls.

"ALISON!" He yelled it at the top of his voice, people looking round in astonishment. But she did not seem to hear him. He pushed his way through the throng, shoving people out of his way where necessary. A few curses were sent in his direction, but he did not care. He needed to get to her.

"ALISON!"

Her head flicked round, surprise on her face. The half-formed smile of recognition turned to a look of concern.

"Alison! Thank goodness…"

"Um, hello Danny, what are you doing here?"

"No time to explain. Do you speak Polish?"

"A little. My grandfather…"

But she never finished her sentence, Danny was already dragging her towards the young man in the fluorescent vest.

"Translate this. Word for word."

"Er…okay!" Alison was starting to look scared. Not as scared as she'd be in a minute, though, Danny thought.

"Okay. Tell him: the Police have found something suspicious…"

Alison broke in.

"I don't know the word for suspicious."

Danny bit his lip.

"Tell him the police have found a bomb in one of the huts. Tell him I will show him to the place."

Alison was gaping at him. Horrified. Speechless.

"Tell him!"

She turned and blurted out a few words, pausing and stuttering a little, but eventually getting the message across.

Danny grabbed Alison by the shoulder, staring into

her blue eyes.

"Now, we don't want a panic, so keep this to yourself. But I'd gather your friends and get out of here if I were you!"

She nodded dumbly, like a lost child. Immobile.

"Go!"

She turned uncertainly, then began to run.

"Okay, now you…" Danny grabbed the official by the arm, "Come with me!"

★ ★ ★

"So…no bomb squad," stated Angus.

"No. It would take them too long to get here. I will have to disarm the bomb myself."

"Do you know how to disarm a bomb?"

"Yes."

"Really?" Angus was a difficult man to lie to.

"My training was a few years ago and I have not used it since, but I can remember quite well."

"Hmm. Well there's not much else we can do but have a go. Let me know what I can do to help."

"There is nothing you can do here. You must…"

"I'm not leaving…"

"Shut up and listen for a minute!"

Angus stopped talking, surprised; he wasn't used to people telling him to shut up.

"There will be two parts to the trigger mechanism for this bomb — the detonator," she pointed at the black box, "and a remote trigger. Maric will have this trigger on his person. You must find Maric and try to stop him using that trigger. While you do this, I will try to disarm the detonator here. Let us hope that one of us succeeds!"

Angus hesitated. It went against everything he believed in to leave Silberstein alone with the bomb, but he knew she was talking sense. He would be of little practical help if he stayed. If he could find Maric, however, and stop him using his remote trigger, then that would be just as effective as disarming the bomb here in the attic.

"What will the trigger look like?" he asked.

"Hard to say. It may be a radio device, but these days it is more likely that he will simply use his mobile phone. Inside the detonator here, will probably be another mobile phone that has been adapted to send an electric current through the detonator charge. All he has to do is use his mobile phone to call the phone in the detonator and... bang!"

Angus thought for a moment.

"Chances are, Maric has gone back downriver in his cabin-cruiser – I'll need to borrow your boat."

Silberstein threw Angus the ignition keys.

"Take care of it. I'll need to fill out a thousand forms if it gets damaged..."

They were interrupted by the clatter of someone climbing the stepladder below. A white face atop fluorescent yellow shoulders popped up through the hatchway. The official's eyes widened immediately into glassy circles of fear and wonder. His jaw worked up and down noiselessly, evidently in an attempt to form some sort of coherent sentence. His hand moved slowly from the edge of the hatch and a finger uncurled shakily in the direction of the canisters. At last, he managed to stammer out a single word:

"B... B... Bomb!"

"Yes, thanks," said Angus. "We are aware of that."

Silberstein took charge, rapping out a brief list of orders. The man nodded at each instruction, repeatedly eyeing the canisters and licking his lips nervously. A final gruff dismissal and he was gone.

"You think he'll get it right?" Angus asked Silberstein doubtfully, as Danny appeared through the hatchway and crawled over to them.

"Yes. They have very detailed plans to follow for

circumstances like these. I just told him to speak to the most senior official and to follow their instructions for an evacuation. And to make sure everyone moves as far from the camp as possible."

"How are you getting on?" asked Danny.

Silberstein smiled. It was the kind of question she might expect if she was doing a crossword puzzle.

"I was just telling your uncle to go and look for Maric, to try and stop him using the remote trigger."

"Aye, you were indeed! Come on Danny, you'd better come with me!"

"Good luck!" said Silberstein.

"Aye. You too," replied Angus, and they were gone.

CHAPTER ELEVEN

As Danny and Angus emerged into the daylight, a grey haired man in a fluorescent vest was giving instructions through a megaphone. What he was saying they could only guess, but he spoke calmly and authoritatively, as though what he was asking was purely a matter of routine, but very necessary nonetheless. As a result, an orderly evacuation was proceeding slowly but surely through various gates in the compound.

"Shouldn't they be moving a bit quicker?" asked Danny, the concern stretching his voice into a thin whisper. "They'll take ages to get everyone out at this rate."

Moreover, those who had made their exit appeared to be gathering just outside the gates, like office workers during a fire drill. He stared at them in frustration.

"They need to be a mile away!" he called after Angus, who was now twenty metres ahead and running for the river. More instructions echoed metallically across the compound and the grey haired man waved his arms to indicate that those outside should keep moving. Danny could see people shrugging and asking questions of each other. He realised that if these thousands of people were more than a few hundred metres from the camp by the time the bomb was set off, it would be a miracle. Shaking his head, he swore and raced after Angus.

Angus was already turning the key in the ignition when Danny leapt aboard the patrol boat. The engine coughed into life and they surged forward through the brown water of the river. Seconds later, they were tearing along at full throttle, the engine roaring and the water hissing as they ripped a ragged white line across it.

The banks flashed past in a blur; the occasional house or industrial building appearing briefly between the bushes and trees. Bridges rushed overhead like vast pterodactyls, casting momentary shadows over them as they hurtled wildly through the long, swooping bends of the river.

Danny leaned over the bows, searching for their quarry amongst the reeds and inlets along the shore. Suddenly, he saw something ahead. A long, dark object — a sinister shadow in the water. He realised too late what it was. A heavy log, at least two metres long, drifting slowly downstream. They were moving so fast he did not have time to react. One second he saw it, the next he realised what it was — and the one after that, they were upon it.

They were lucky; it missed them by a few centimetres, bouncing harmlessly past in the bow wave to their left. If it had hit them it would have torn a hole in their boat that would have sunk them in seconds. Danny turned and shouted at Angus.

"We're going too fast!"

"WHAT?!"

The noise of the engine was drowning out their words.

"WE ARE GOING TOO FAST!" he yelled, trying desperately to make himself heard. "WE'LL END UP HITTING SOMETHING!"

Angus grinned.

"CHEESE AND SALAMI!" he shouted back.

Danny peered at his uncle suspiciously, then sighed. If Angus had decided on full throttle, there wasn't much point in arguing with him.

As they rounded the next bend, however,

their search came to an end. On the right hand bank, tied up to a derelict jetty, they saw a small, white cabin-cruiser — the same one they had seen on the bend of the river below the Wawel. For a moment, Angus hoped they might take their enemy by surprise, but the noise of their boat had clearly alerted them. One of Maric's shaven-headed henchmen appeared on the afterdeck and hurriedly cast off. Maric appeared next, jumping behind the controls and starting the engine.

The cruiser was soon under way and accelerating fast, but it didn't stand a chance of escaping. The police boat had an enormous outboard engine and was designed for just this sort of thing — the high speed pursuit of criminals. In comparison, the cabin-cruiser was like a tortoise with a gammy hip.

"GET BACK HERE AND TAKE THE WHEEL!" shouted Angus.

"EH?!"

"TAKE THE WHEEL!"

"BUT..." Danny stopped; he realised that this was no time to argue. He jumped down from the bows and ran back to where Angus stood.

"Here you go." Angus indicated the wheel.

"Get me as close as you can to Maric's boat. I'm going to jump in and have a go at getting the trigger from Maric."

"Are you nuts! There are three of them!"

"No choice, mate."

Danny knew that this was the simple truth. For Angus, there was no alternative. When people's lives were at risk, turning round and running away wasn't an option. You took the cards life dealt you, and you always did the right thing — regardless of the consequences. There was no other way to live.

They were almost upon them now. Danny could feel the spray from the other boat on his face. He wondered if they had guns. Certainly nobody had shot at them yet.

"CLOSER!" shouted Angus. How could he get any closer? They were already just a couple of metres from the other boat. The thug who stood in the back of it was so close Danny could read his tattoos. He had picked up a boat hook and was preparing to swing it at Angus.

"CLOSER!"

The only way he could get any closer was to ram the other boat. Angus turned and glowered at Danny.

"DAMMIT DANNY! GET CLOSER!"

Danny shrugged.

"Okay!"

He swung the wheel hard to the left, causing the patrol boat to yaw suddenly. There was a violent bang, followed by a squeal, as they hit the cabin-cruiser amidships. At this moment Angus leapt — straight into the path of the swinging boat hook. Its wooden handle shattered across Angus's shoulder, but that did not slow him down. A fraction of a second later, Angus's right fist shot out in a vicious hook. It connected neatly with the thug's temple, causing him to stagger. Angus followed it up with a nose-breaking jab. A second right hook knocked the insensible thug overboard. The whole fight had taken just three seconds.

It was far from over, however, as the second of Maric's henchmen had appeared from the cabin. The thug grinned — a lopsided leer of broken teeth in a face like a sack full of rocks. It was the brute who had been with Maric on that filthy night in Dunkeld and he hadn't grown any more handsome in the interim. He looked big and tough, but his movements were slow and lumbering. Angus knew what he had to do.

"Float like a butterfly!" he shouted at the thug.

"Eh?"

Jab. Cross. Right hook. Left hook. Left hook… hard right hook!

That hard right hook broke three bones in Angus's hand — and knocked a second Neo-Nazi over the side.

"Sting like a bee!" Angus called after him, as he toppled into the water.

At the moment he said 'bee', the engine of the cabin-cruiser died. From raucous noise one moment to a curious silence the next. Turning, Angus saw that Maric was no longer steering the boat, but had turned off the ignition and was now glaring in his direction. As the boat glided slowly to a halt, Maric began to advance on him.

Angus dropped into a defensive stance, sideways on to his opponent and arms raised in front of him. Maric stood upright, arms by his sides, as though Angus posed no threat to him at all. Suddenly, he laughed.

"Well done! You have made, ah… quick work

of my men."

"Aye. You might as well give up now, before I kick your arse too."

Maric smiled and pretended to inspect his finger nails.

"You will find me a rather more…"

CRACK!

The blow came so quickly Angus did not have time to react. He was aware of a flash of movement… then a sudden pain in his temple. He staggered backwards, trying stay upright… the world swayed sickeningly for a moment. Maric was clearly an expert in hand to hand combat. Angus had never fought anyone who could move as fast as this.

He saw the next blow coming — a straight jab — and rocked backwards to avoid it. He stepped forward with a jab of his own, but Maric side-stepped it easily. A stab of agony exploded in his knee and he fell to the floor. As he struggled to his feet, he saw the toe of a boot swing towards his face. A light seemed to flash between his eyes and he was thrown backwards to the deck again. Stunned.

Angus shook his head, trying to focus. Trying to stay conscious. As he did so he heard a laugh and looked up. Maric was standing over him, holding something in his hand — a small rectangle of black plastic. It was a mobile phone.

"Want to kill some Jews?" he asked, waving the phone at him. "I have an app for that."

As he said it, he pressed his thumb to the phone's touch screen and looked up at the sky, as though listening for something. A brief silence — then, in the distance, a deep and ominous 'THUMP!'.

Angus knew what it was. He'd heard the sound too many times in his life to be mistaken. His head swam and he could taste the bile in the back of his throat. He had failed. After all their efforts, Maric had won. Thousands of people would, at this very moment, be fighting for their lives against the most lethal nerve-agent man had ever devised. They would die horrible, protracted deaths — all because of his failure.

A wave of nausea swept over him and his vision blurred — he was slipping into unconsciousness. As he waited for the final blows to come, the world went dark and there was a terrible roaring in his ears.

★ ★ ★

At the moment Angus had jumped into Maric's boat,

Danny had been gripping the wheel of the patrol boat like his life depended on it. As the two boats had crashed into each other, Danny had fallen to the floor, still holding desperately to the wheel. As he had fallen, he had dragged the wheel to the right, and the boat had peeled off in that direction, still tearing along at full throttle.

Staggering to his feet, Danny realised he was now heading straight for the riverbank and was moments from smashing into it. Going at the speed he was, hitting it would undoubtedly involve loud noises, screaming and, very probably, a certain amount of premature dying on his part. He snatched the wheel to the left and the boat lurched round in a sudden turn that threw a curtain of white foam into the air.

Danny swore under his breath.

Now he had a different problem. He was roaring downriver at a phenomenal speed, with no idea what he was doing. He knew what the wheel did, of course, that was obvious, but the other buttons and levers were a mystery to him. His first priority was to slow the damn thing down.

It was almost impossible to work out what to do. He couldn't study the controls in detail because he had to concentrate so hard on steering the boat. The river twisted and turned endlessly; take his eyes off the steering for a couple of seconds and he would bury himself into the bank in an environmentally unfriendly exploding fireball.

Glancing down for the third time he saw a chrome lever with a polished wooden handle and remembered that Angus had pushed this lever forward shortly after starting the boat. Taking one hand off the steering wheel he gingerly pulled it back towards himself. Immediately the roar of the engine became less deafening and the bows dropped a little — the boat was slowing down. He had guessed correctly that it was the throttle control.

Danny heaved a long sigh of relief and pulled the lever right back. The speed of the boat dropped quickly to just a few knots and the bellow of the engine fell to a quiet rumble. He did not waste time congratulating himself, however. Spinning the wheel hard left, he turned the boat round and pointed it back upstream.

He had no idea how Angus had fared after jumping into Maric's boat. He could easily have been killed by now. Or, just possibly, he might have managed to beat up all three thugs so as to stop them setting off the bomb. Equally, he might, at this very moment, be fighting for his life and in desperate need of assistance. Danny took a deep breath and pushed the throttle lever as far forward as it would go.

The boat surged forward and the engine noise rose again to a deafening roar. This was it, the moment of truth. What would he find when he got back to the cabin-cruiser? Would he find Angus triumphant — or would he find Maric laughing over his uncle's corpse? And if Maric had won, what could he, Danny, possibly do about it? What could he do that Angus could not?

These questions whirled around in his head as he tore upriver, his knuckles white from gripping the wheel. At last, he rounded a bend and saw the cabin-cruiser ahead, drifting slowly downriver with its engine off. At first he could make out nothing more, but as he drew closer he saw a tall figure with dark hair standing in the back of it.

"Oh, no!"

It was a horrified whisper that barely escaped his lips. The figure was Nikola Maric. He seemed to be laughing. He was holding something up. Danny was too far away to see what the object was, but knew instinctively that it was the trigger! Maric was about to blow up the poison gas!

Danny knew what he must do. Now he realised what he could do that Angus could not.

The patrol boat was flying — barely kissing the water with its hull as its huge engine flung it forwards. Danny held the wheel hard, scared that the speed might tear it from his hands. The cruiser was barely a hundred metres away. Maric was waving the trigger, as though showing it to someone in the bottom of the boat. Danny held his course — pointing the bows of the patrol boat straight at Maric. Maric might be tougher than him, but Danny would bet burgers to broccoli that he wasn't tougher than half a ton of police patrol boat.

At fifty metres Danny saw Maric straighten and gaze up at the sky. A split second later, Maric's head snapped round and he stared wide-eyed in Danny's direction. There was no time for action. The patrol boat covered those last few metres so fast Maric didn't even have time to blink.

The cabin-cruiser, that had seemed so small and flimsy from afar, suddenly seemed as tall and as solid as a brick wall. Danny had no idea what would happen when the boats hit each other. Perhaps the patrol boat was tough enough to crash right through the cruiser and he would be okay? Or perhaps the two boats would explode in a gigantic fireball, vaporising all of them in an instant? He was about to find out.

A brutal, tearing crash split the air. The cracking of wood, the squeal of plastic and the groan of metal cried out together in a deafening cacophony as the two boats collided. Danny felt his boat rise under him — a sudden wave of energy punching up through his legs and into his body. His knees buckled and his head momentarily smashed forwards into the steering wheel.

However, it didn't stop him. The next thing he knew, he was out of the boat and tumbling through the air. He saw brief moments in time — the wreckage of the two boats below him — a heavy sky of grey clouds — trees spinning past — dark water approaching.

He smacked heavily into the river, the impact knocking the breath from him. But he was underwater only briefly; thrashing his way to the surface in a few seconds. He found himself surrounded by wreckage — pieces of timber and plastic floating all around him. It was as though the cabin-cruiser had simply disintegrated into a thousand fragments. The police boat hadn't fared much better — its shattered hull was slowly sinking below the surface twenty metres away.

"ANGUS!" he shouted, hardly daring to hope that his uncle might still be alive. If Maric had not already killed Angus, then it seemed likely that Danny had done the job for him. Surely no one in the cabin-cruiser could have survived such a crash? Danny looked around; there was no sign of his uncle or Maric. An eerie silence had descended over the river.

"ANGUS!" Danny yelled again.

All Danny could hear was the gentle rustling of the wind in the trees. Then, among the wreckage, he saw something that made his heart lurch. It was the body of a dark-haired man – floating face down in the river.

"ANGUS!"

He thrashed through the water, desperate to cover the distance between them. Reaching the body, he grabbed it by the shoulder and pulled it over. It rolled slowly, like the carcass of a whale caught in the surf. An arm flopped heavily into the water as it turned. Danny stared at the deathly white face in front of him.

It was Nikola Maric.

He looked around once more, hoping to spot Angus, but it was difficult to see anything amongst the debris. He could be behind – or under – any of the ragged pieces of hull floating around him. Or, of course, he could be at the bottom of the river…

Grabbing Maric by his collar, he swam as quickly as he could manage to the shore, dragging the body behind him. Clawing his way up the muddy bank, he pulled Maric onto the dew-soaked grass. Reaching down he placed his fingers on the thug's neck, just below the jawline, and felt for a pulse. Nothing… or was there? He repositioned his fingers a little. Yes! There it was — the faintest tremor under the skin, a pulse so weak he could barely feel it.

Thrusting a hand into his trouser pocket, Danny pulled out his smart phone. It was ruined of course, the water had seeped in and fried its electrics. A phone that until five minutes ago could do pretty much anything, now served only one purpose. He wiped the lifeless screen on a piece of litter, doing his best to get it dry, then held it close to Maric's nose and mouth. The tiniest hint of condensation appeared as a grey mist on the glass, then faded away. A few seconds later, it appeared again. Maric, against all the odds, was still breathing.

"You lucky son of a…"

Danny fell to his knees, exhausted. He suddenly noticed how cold he was and shivered as a fresh wind bit through his wet clothes. His head throbbed and a stabbing pain began to build in his left knee. As the adrenaline subsided, his body was letting him know just how much damage he had done to himself.

"Okay, got to get moving," he muttered. "Must find Angus…"

As he rose, however, he heard a quiet, strained voice behind him. The voice of someone fighting severe pain.

"Remind me never to let you drive the Hi-Lux."

Danny's head snapped round, a smile on his lips even before his eyes found him. There was no mistaking that voice – it was Angus!

Danny splashed into the water, reaching out to help his uncle ashore.

"Aah…haaargh! Careful lad… I think that one's broken. Angus winced as Danny let go and grabbed his other arm.

"That's better. Thanks Danny…" Angus paused mid-sentence as they clambered together from the river. His gaze had fallen on the unconscious figure of Nikola Maric.

"Blimey, Danny, did you…?" A new respect was etched into Angus's face.

"Actually, I just found him floating in the water. But if anybody asks, you can tell them I kung-fu'd his Nazi ass."

Angus laughed, then winced again.

"I'll make sure it goes in the Police report," he said, with a grin.

"And the newspaper article?"

"Oh, no. Some things are sacred!"

Danny looked down at Nikola Maric, the dangerous lunatic they had chased the length and breadth of Europe — the man whose terrible plot had come so close to succeeding. A sudden doubt popped into his head.

"We did stop him, didn't we?" he asked. "We did get to him in time?"

Angus's grey eyes darkened and the muscles in his jaw stiffened, as if a hideous memory had suddenly returned to haunt him. Danny knew what that look on his uncle's face meant.

CHAPTER TWELVE

What Silberstein had not told them was that her 'training' in bomb disposal had been a two day selection course for the Warsaw Police Department Bomb Disposal Unit. Unfortunately, while she had proven herself an able student, the department psychiatrist had evaluated her as 'emotionally unsuited to the rigours of bomb disposal' and she had been turned down. She had suspected he'd really meant '*women* are emotionally unsuited to the rigours of bomb disposal' and had considered making a complaint of sexual discrimination. In the end, she had decided to let it drop and had forgotten all about it. Until now.

She tried desperately to remember what she had learnt during that selection course, but it had been years ago and most of the time had been taken up with intelligence and initiative tests. She realised she would just have to do her best. Tackle it slowly and methodically — and try not to blow herself up.

★ ★ ★

The crates had been arranged in a triangle around the explosive charge and heavy steel plates had been welded over the top of each one to prevent removal of the cylinders. She knew that the explosive charge was a block of C4 and that the black plastic box would be the detonator. A mysterious length of red electrical wire emerged from one side of the detonator, wound its way around the crates and then disappeared back into it on its opposite side. She wasn't sure what this could be.

She decided that the best thing would be to get into that plastic box. However, as it had no lid or access panel, she would have to cut her way in. One of the leather pouches on her belt held a 'multi-tool' — the kind of modern alternative to a Swiss Army knife that incorporated a pair of pliers. Pulling it out she opened the cutting blade, took a deep breath, and gave the box an experimental prod. Nothing.

She gave it a harder poke. The plastic flexed a little, but the sharp blade of her tool left only the tiniest mark. She could feel her heart thumping, reminding her that she was alive and how easily that could change. She pushed harder. Then harder still. The blade went in another fraction of a millimetre.

She could tell the plastic was not thick by the way it flexed when she tried to pierce it, but it was hard. Any attempt to cut into it would inevitably be a brutal, forceful affair, far too vigorous for a situation like this, when the utmost delicacy was required. She sat back, staring at the device in front of her, trying to figure a way around the problem.

Think, think, think…

Suddenly, she snapped her fingers and began searching through the pouches on her belt again. They held all sorts of things that she found useful in her day-to-day police work: a notebook, first aid kit, dog biscuits, sticky tape, whistle… somewhere in there was a cigarette lighter.

Finding it, she flicked it on and held the flame under the blade of her multi-tool. It went black with soot and then began to smoke. After about twenty seconds she gave the box another experimental prod with the blade. It went in much more easily this time, the hot steel melting through the plastic like butter. She was now able to cut a slit in the plastic about a centimetre long before the blade cooled down and had to be held over the flame again. Repeating the procedure, she made painstaking progress. At last, after what seemed like an agonisingly long time, she had cut a rectangular hole in the side of the box.

Using Angus's torch, she examined the detonator's interior. What she saw horrified her – a confusing mass of wires and electrical components. She felt a brief wave of panic rise in her chest, but fought it back.

Stay calm. Stay focused.

She looked again — there were a few things she recognised. To the left was a battery, a tangle of wires and a shiny metal tube. Silberstein knew that this was the blasting cap and that the other end of it would be buried deep into the explosive to the rear of the box.

On the right was what appeared to be the insides of a mobile phone. The outer casing and key-pad had been removed, but the circuit board, screen and battery remained. Tucked behind the innards of the mobile phone was another circuit board. The ends of the red electrical wire that was wrapped around the crates were attached to it.

Silberstein wondered briefly if she could simply remove the battery from the mobile phone, meaning it would be unable to receive a signal. Wouldn't that prevent Maric from detonating the bomb? On closer inspection, however, she saw that the components had been securely bonded together with large globs of epoxy glue.

Next, she inspected the blasting cap. It was connected by a multitude of wires to the mobile phone, the battery and to a pair of small rectangular electrical components whose purpose was a mystery. What if she cut the wrong wire? Would the bomb go off? That was what happened in the movies — would it happen in real life? Silberstein realised that any attempt she made to diffuse the detonator would be guesswork – a wild stab in the dark that could have tragic consequences, and not only for herself.

Don't panic! Keep thinking logically. There must be a way round this…

There was only one thing she could do; she would have to disconnect the bomb from the crates and get it as far from the canisters as possible before Maric detonated it. She would only have to get it a short distance — perhaps fifty metres — before the canisters would be safe from the explosion. Of course, if she was still holding it when Maric set it off, she would be vaporised. She glanced at her watch. Eight minutes to nine. Not much time.

The C4 was fixed to one of the crates using duct tape. That, at least, would be easy to deal with. The problem was the long, red wire that snaked its way sinuously through the metal latticework of the crates. There was no way of getting the bomb away from the crates without cutting that wire.

Taking another look at the circuit board to which the wire was attached, Silberstein realised its purpose — it was to stop anyone moving the bomb away from the crates. An electric current would be running through that wire and as soon as it was cut the electric current would stop. Which would trigger the detonator…

Keep calm! Breathe…

She needed to find a way of cutting the wire without breaking the current. She looked at her watch again. Seven minutes to nine.

A short circuit!

If the electric current could travel along a different wire then the red wire could be cut without triggering the detonator! Silberstein pulled out the contents of her pouches and spread them across the floor in front of her.

Zip-ties, dog-biscuits, notebook, pencil, handcuffs, whistle, sticky tape, first aid kit… but no wire.

She pulled open her first aid kit desperately, already knowing the answer. Bandages, antiseptic, painkillers... a forlorn pile of useless junk. If only she had her iPod.

Time was ticking away: an inexorable slide towards massacre. Five minutes to nine.

Silberstein stared, her mind stuck.

Stalled.

Frozen.

Mentally unsuited to the rigours...

NOTEBOOK!

She snatched it up. Along the top edge of the small, blue book, was a spiral binding; a long white coil that held the pages together. Peering closely at the end of the binding she saw a barely visible gleam under the white plastic coating – the spiral binding was made of wire!

She flicked open her multi-tool and using the pliers grabbed one end of the binding. Pulling hard, she ripped it from the book, sending shreds of white paper everywhere. She then used the tool to strip the plastic coating from the ends of wire.

This might just work...

She turned to the detonator and the wire that wound its way round the crates and pulled out the cutting blade of her multi-tool. At a point about three centimetres from the detonator she cut carefully into the red plastic insulation, exposing the copper wire underneath. She then did the same to the wire entering the other side of the detonator.

She checked her watch. Four minutes to nine.

Taking the spiral binding of the notebook, she now attached one end of it to one of the exposed sections of copper wire by twisting it round with her pliers. Holding her breath, she brought the other end of the binding up to the exposed section on the other side of the detonator. When it came into contact, it would complete the circuit and the electric current ought to be able to run through the binding. Which would mean that she could cut the red wire without blowing herself up and killing thousands of innocent people.

She brought it closer. Once more, she held her breath. Closer, closer, closer... she had contact.

Something clicked faintly in the detonator.

Oh God! What was that! What the... Stay calm! Stay calm!

She could clearly hear the ticking of her wristwatch in the crushing silence. The seconds thumped by – a terrifying countdown to carnage.

Nothing happened.

It was going to work! She twisted the binding securely into place. Only one thing left to do: cut the red wire.

Suddenly and unexpectedly, a feeling of confidence swept over her. She was in control. She was going to succeed. She might not be a bomb disposal expert, but she was a damned fine police officer and she was going to save these people's lives even if she died trying.

Quite calmly, she leant forward and snipped the red wire in two. No unpleasant noises came from the detonator.

Quickly, she tore off the duct tape which secured the bomb to the crate and eased it away, the red wire sliding harmlessly through the steel latticework. She had done it! The bomb was free of the VX!

Another glance at her watch. One minute to nine. Maric might trigger the bomb at any moment. She hurried to the hatch, cradling the heavy lump of C4 in her arms like a venomous baby. Easing herself carefully down the stepladder, she broke into a run as soon as she hit the floor.

She pounded through the hut and out of the door — sprinting across the tarmac towards the river. The camp was almost empty, but there were still a few people queuing at the gates, and there seemed to be many hundreds milling around not far from the wire. What were those stupid officials playing at?

Suddenly aware of something to her right she looked round. It was Hugo, bounding along at her side, ears and tongue flapping in the wind and his crossed eyes shining. The poor thing had no idea of the danger. He thought it was all just a game.

She reached the hole in the fence and scrambled through on all fours. People were staring at her. Pointing. Raised voices. Not far now…

'Dit-Dee… Dit-Dee… Dit-Deee…'

A mobile phone. Not hers…

Oh… HELL!

Still several metres from the riverbank, she hurled the bomb with all her might. She saw it sail through the air – an angular black lump against the grey sky. It fell towards the water…

She heard nothing. She felt nothing. A supersonic explosion. Over before she could know it had happened.

They followed him down a long, brightly lit corridor,

thumping through heavy fire-doors and following a crimson line painted on the floor. He was a hunched figure in an immaculate lab coat and so short Danny could look down on the white island of skin atop his balding, bullet-shaped head.

"The next twelve hours are critical," said the doctor, turning a corner and taking them down another dazzling corridor, still following the blood-red line on the grey linoleum.

"She is very weak. She lost a lot of blood. Punctured lung. Broken legs. Ruptured spleen."

He paused outside a white door with a wired glass window.

"Her father has been informed. He cannot get here before the morning. I hope he will be in time." He grimaced, sighed and gestured towards the door. "In there." And with that, he turned and shuffled off, back in the direction of the emergency ward.

Danny and Angus peered through the window. Silberstein lay on her back, tightly wrapped in white linen sheets. The skin of her face and arms was a mottled sea of brown, black, purple and yellow. Her eyes, nose and lips were so swollen she was almost unrecognisable. A clear plastic tube disappeared up her nose and another led from her bandaged arm to a bag of fluid suspended from a pole. Danny felt Angus's hand on his shoulder for the second time that day.

Taking a seat either side of Silberstein's bed, they sat down to wait. Whatever happened, they would be there with her. Danny looked at his watch. It was 5 pm. They could wait all night.

Not long after midnight Danny felt his head droop towards his chest and he rose, rubbing his eyes and shaking himself awake. Angus sat staring stonily at the wall opposite, as motionless as a statue. Danny wondered what he was thinking. He was about to ask, but stopped himself and wandered over to the window instead.

Pulling back the curtain he peered out at the night sky. The clouds had gone, leaving a clear sky of bright stars. He stood there for a long time, watching the constellations rotate in their slow, inexorable procession around the Pole Star. At last, with his feet beginning to ache, he returned to his chair. Shortly afterwards, despite his best efforts, he was sound asleep.

★ ★ ★

He woke as the first light of dawn crept in a pale yellow tide across the walls of the room. There was no noise at all, save for the breathing of the woman beside him. Angus stood by the window, taking his turn staring at the sky.

Danny closed his eyes again, and listened to Silberstein's breathing. Was he imagining it, or was it a little deeper, a little stronger than it had been last night? He looked across at her, hoping for some sign that she was on the mend, but she looked as fragile and as broken as ever.

Her hand lay close to his on the white bed sheets. It was small and delicate, much smaller than Danny's own hands, which were large for a boy of his age and covered with the cuts and calluses of mountain biking and climbing. He reached over and slipped his fingers over hers, giving them a squeeze.

He nearly jumped out of his skin when she groaned and her fingers grasped his in return. In shock, he drew his hand away, terrified that he might have hurt her. But she did not groan again.

Instead, her head rolled slowly to face him and,

after a few deep breaths, her eyes flickered open. Her eyes were bloodshot and the pupils were dilated into black pools, like the dark waters of a subterranean lake. Her lips twitched and she whispered,

"Hugo?"

"He's fine. Although, I think he might be even more cross-eyed than before…"

"And Maric?"

"We got him, but not until he'd triggered the bomb. You saved thousands of lives. It is a good thing you did that bomb disposal training!"

Silberstein's head dropped back onto her pillow and a tear ran suddenly from the corner of her eye. Then she did something he was not expecting — she laughed.

"My bomb disposal training!"

A giggle, a wheezing cough and wince. Then a tired, but genuine, smile.

Danny looked at her, puzzled. It had to be the painkillers. Why else would she find that funny?

Danny and Angus walked slowly across the parking lot in the warm spring sunshine. They were both

limping and Angus's right arm was in a sling across his chest. Climbing stiffly into the Hi-Lux, Danny looked across at his uncle.

"Are you going to be able to drive okay? It's a long way to Dunkeld."

"Och, aye. It's only a fractured ulna and three broken fingers!"

As Angus pulled the car keys from his pocket, his phone buzzed to indicate he had received an email. As he read it, his eyebrows climbed towards his hairline and the corner of his mouth turned upwards in a lopsided smile.

"Hey, Danny." There was a hint of disbelief in his voice. "Update from Newby. You remember I emailed him the photos of the paintings that I took in Maric's study? He's just heard back from the Art and Antiques Unit. Apparently they were listed as having been stolen by the Nazis during the war. That's no great surprise – we guessed as much. The big news is this – one of the pictures was a Rembrandt!"

"A Rembrandt! Even I've heard of him! Aren't his pictures worth a fortune?"

"Millions! Even on the black market it would be worth a huge amount! Newby says that the

Art and Antiques Unit are now working with the Russian Police to try and recover the paintings from the gangsters."

Danny sat back in his seat and smiled.

"I wonder what Knut would make of all this?" he said, remembering the old Norwegian agent who had started them on their adventure. "Will you send him a copy of your article for *The Times*?"

Angus grinned, a twinkle in his grey eyes.

"I think we can do better than that! I think we should go and see him in Norway- tell him our story in person. Let him know that your great-grandfather wasn't the last heroic Lansing to fight the Nazis!"

Danny flushed a little, before replying.

"And I suppose if our mountaineering kit should somehow get packed in with our luggage, that would just be a lucky coincidence?"

Angus turned the key in the ignition and threw the Hi-Lux into gear. Then he turned to Danny and winked.

"You are developing into a fine thinker, my lad."

ACKNOWLEDGEMENTS

A big thanks to my wife Marie, who is unfailingly supportive and looks better than any woman I know in a beanie and down jacket. Thanks to my Mum for her proof-reading and to my Dad for lending me 'Two Eggs On My Plate' and 'The Shetland Bus', the books that sparked my interest in the Norwegian Resistance. Many thanks also to Keith Charters for his skilled and sympathetic editing and to Lawrence Mann for another brilliant cover!

–Matt Cartney

The Sons of Rissouli
(Book 1 in the Danny Lansing series)

ISBN 978-1-905537-21-1 (paperback, RRP £6.99)

When Danny Lansing goes to live with his cool Uncle Angus, he knows life will never be the same again. But he doesn't expect to be catapulted into a world of guns, explosions and high-speed chases.

After they uncover a top-secret, highly illegal operation to ship arms out of the country, Danny and Angus race to North Africa to investigate. As they pursue the bloodthirsty Sons of Rissouli across country the stakes get higher, and Danny is thrown into dangers he could never have imagined.

He'll have to be tough enough to survive in the brutal furnace of the desert. But when another life is at stake, will he have the guts to risk his own?

There's no doubt about it. It's going to be an adventure...

The Cat Kin

ISBN 978-1-905537-16-7 (paperback, RRP £6.99)

Everyone who came to the strange gym class was looking for something else. What they found was the mysterious Mrs Powell and Pashki, a lost art from an age when cats were worshipped as gods.

Ben and Tiffany wonder: who is their eccentric old teacher? What does she really want with them? And why are they suddenly able to see in the dark?

Meanwhile, in London's gloomy streets, human vermin are stirring. Ben and Tiffany may soon be glad of their new gifts. But against men whose cunning is matched only by their unspeakable cruelty, will even nine lives be enough?